DANGEROUS WATERS

Paul Collins

Publisher: WriteAdvice Press (Alberta, Canada)

Editor: Mr. Ted Williams, Freelance Editor

Cover Design and Interior Format by: The Killion Group
http://thekilliongroupinc.com

Paperback ISBN: 978-0-9878918-8-4
Anniversary edition

To Caitlin, Ryan, and Keira

"In war, whichever side may call itself the victor, there are no winners, but all are losers."
-Neville Chamberlain
British Prime Minister 1937-1940

Newfoundland 1942

BRITAIN'S OLDEST COLONY IN THE NEW WORLD, this storm-battered island in the Western Atlantic was surrounded by *der Führer's* U-boats, trying to sever her lifelines along with Mother England's.

Isolated and under siege by the forces of Nazi Germany; coveted by both Canada and the United States, Newfoundland was the "Gibraltar of America." But to the men of the small corvettes, minesweepers, and patrol boats of the mostly volunteer Royal Canadian Navy, St. John's, Newfoundland's capital city and home port of the Newfoundland Escort Force

(NEF) was known fondly as *Newfyjohn.*

This is a story from the *Battle of the Atlantic.* About ships' sinkings and spies. Sabotage and commando raids. Death and daring escapes. But it is also the story of two people finding the most basic of human emotions...love...in a world gone mad.

AUTHOR'S NOTE

This book is a work of fiction and I've taken a lot of liberties historically, procedurally, and technologically. It is, however, based on actual events and people, and several of the names are real. They were used to add authenticity to the story but the actions and motives of these individuals as depicted here are, again, pure fiction. I hope you *Battle of the Atlantic* purists out there will forgive me.

The basic story is true.

In the early hours of November 2, 1942, a German *Unterseeboot* entered the anchorage at Wabana, Bell Island - for the second time in three months - and sank two ships, with tragic loss of life, as well as severely damaging the Scotia Pier. A Royal Canadian Navy (RCN) corvette, HMCS *Drumheller*, was patrolling the Bay that morning, as were two Fairmile patrol boats. Rumours abounded at the time that there was a spy involved but an investigation by the authorities failed to uncover one. My own investigations reveal that there was actually an Abwehr spy on board the U-boat, destined for the Gaspé Peninsula, Quebec. He was caught shortly after landing and turned into a double agent.

Of two attempted missions to land automated weather stations on Canada's east coast, only one succeeded:. *U537* did land and install a weather station - code named "Kurt"- on October 22, 1943, at what is now called Martin's Bay. The other U-boat, *U867*, was sunk en route, with the captain's body eventually washing ashore in Norway.

In late 1942, the *Knights of Columbus* hostel in St. John's was burned to the ground, with great loss of life. It was one of several major fires which occurred in the City during the War, all attributed to arson. While no one was ever charged, rumours persist that, in 1943, a Nazi radio was discovered on the Southside Hills overlooking Kilbride, and the perpetrator caught.

Joseph Prim, a Second World War merchant Captain, and author Mike

McCarthy supplied the plotline for the *Mary Sullivan* episode in their book *Those in Peril.* The U-boat in the account subsequently sank HMCS *Valleyfield* off the South Coast of Newfoundland along with most of her crew. The late Herb Wells, author of *Under the White Ensign I & II* and *Comrades in Arms I & II,* alleges that the Germans actually did plan a raid on the Torbay Airbase, which is corroborated to some degree by testimony given before a 1944 US Congressional Hearing.

There are many good books which recount the Battle of the Atlantic, and all include the forays into the waters around Newfoundland. Two of the best are *North Atlantic Run* by Marc Milner, and *U-boats Against Canada* by Michael Hadley. Although both are a bit dated now, they are considered classic works by most Canadian naval historians. The late Steve Neary wrote a detailed account of the sinkings at Wabana, entitled *The Enemy on our Doorstep* which is, unfortunately, now out of print.

There have been so many other very good books on Newfoundland's Second World War/*Battle of the Atlantic* experience produced during the twenty years since this novel was originally published that I cannot list them here because it would become a multi-page bibliography. The one exception that I would like to note is the award winning *Occupied St. John's: A Social History of a City at War, 1939-1945,* edited by Steven High. It is well worth reading. Of course, I recommend that you also check out my own *The 'Newfyjohn' Solution: St. John's, Newfoundland as a Case Study in Second World War Allied Naval Base Development During the Battle of the Atlantic.* It's not really a "page turner," but if you want to discover the intricacies of turning a small, poorly defended port into a naval base "of strategic importance" in the middle of a shooting war, you might find it interesting.

The Second World War was a pivotal epoch in our province's history, and precipitated Newfoundland's entry into Confederation with Canada, for good or bad. Whatever your opinion, it is a fascinating time period (at least I think so) and well worth investigating. Rick Stanley of *Ocean Quest Adventures* continues to lead diving expeditions from all over the world to the wrecks at the bottom of Conception Bay, if you are adventurous and want to actually experience Newfoundland's Second World War history *in situ*.

Regardless, I hope you enjoy reading *Dangerous Waters* as much as I did revising it for this edition.

-Paul W Collins

St. John's, September 2015

www.drpaulwcollins.com

PROLOGUE

September 5, 1942
Bell Island, Conception Bay,
Newfoundland

LIKE   SOME   GREAT
PREHISTORIC SHARK, it had lain on
the ocean floor all night. Waiting,
listening, but not sleeping. The strong
rays of the morning sun penetrated
the depths of its hideout but still the
brute did not stir. Activity began
above; small boats traversed the
surface, larger vessels slowly moved
through the anchorage, mooring close
to the Island, anchor chains rattling
as they unwound. It did not leave the
comfort of the seabed. Activity ceased,
as if terminated by the noonday gun
that discharged in the Wabana Town

Square. The beast stirred, ever so slightly. With a shudder, it separated itself from the soft bottom, unseen by those above. The creature approached the surface and stopped just below, waiting.

The thin tip of the periscope pierced the smooth membrane separating the two worlds. Sunlight glinted briefly off the clear glass of the lens as it whirled around, taking in its surroundings. It stopped as it spied one of the moored ships straining at its chain as if sensing its peril. The tube disappeared... then reappeared a second later. A low rumble emanated from below and a fast-moving shadow, trailing effervescence, streaked towards the black, rust-stained hull, 500 yards ahead.

The track intersected with the ship and a geyser of white water grew along her side, higher and higher, until it reached its apex, and then collapsed into itself. The vessel, mortally wounded, settled slowly by the stern, getting lower and lower, until her deck was awash. With a final burst of boiling water, she disappeared from view. But she wasn't dead yet! Inside the U-boat, all hands heard the agonized moaning and tearing as bulkheads collapsed and internal fittings tore from their foundations. A living thing in its final death throes. Eventually, the broken hull impacted the ocean floor, not far from where her killer had lain all night, and was silent. Air bubbles streamed from the jagged hole in her side, upwards to the surface, marking her final resting place.

CHAPTER ONE

OBERLEUTNANT ZUR SEE GERHARD TRÖJER stiffened to attention and executed a regulation naval salute as *Kapitän-Leutnant* Konrad Wassermann crossed the prow to the deck of the *U581*. Behind him in two parallel lines stood those members of the crew not on watch.

Wassermann returned the salute. "Report, *Oberleutnant.*"

"All provisions and ammunition on board. All crew accounted for and the Second Watch are at their stations. *U581* is ready for sea," replied Tröjer.

"Very good. Take us out, *Oberleutnant* Tröjer. I'll be in my cabin." Wassermann turned to go.

"*Kapitän!*" Tröjer hesitated. "Wouldn't you like to address the crew, sir?"

Wassermann turned. "No, why should I, *Leutnant?*"

"Well, sir, it's our first war patrol and most of the men have never seen combat. I just thought a few words of encouragement..." Tröjer trailed off.

"*Leutnant,* the men have been well trained and all know their duty to the *Fatherland.* I should not have to remind them of it." Wassermann paused. "Get under way, *Leutnant.* I assume I can trust you to do that by yourself?"

Without replying, Tröjer turned to dismiss the crew. Wassermann did not react to the slight, not unexpected, but hid his irritation by briskly mounting the *Wintergarten,* the circular bandstand at the rear of the Conning Tower. He reached the Bridge and, after quickly making sure that everything topside was in order, vanished down the hatch. Tröjer gave instructions to the petty officer in charge of the deck to single up all lines. The crew filed past him to the open galley hatch abaft the Conning Tower and quickly disappeared down into the boat – the *Bon Voyage* fanfare of earlier days had long disappeared. Now the once-feared *Grey Wolves* seemed to slink out of harbour, hoping no one would notice.

U581's First Watch Officer climbed the side of the tower to the bridge, patting the stylized *W* as he went. The U-boat's emblem was supposed to represent the first letter of the captain's surname but looked more like the shapely rear-end of some young *Fräulein*. Irreverently, because they really didn't like their *Kaleu* that much, the men had started the custom of patting it, for luck, as they passed.

Tröjer gave orders to release the springs that still held them to the concrete dock, and issued several quick instructions through the voicepipe to the *Zentrale* below. *U581* quietly separated from the quay as the electric motors turned the starboard screw in reverse and the port one ahead. The U-boat pivoted on her axis until her sharp prow pointed out into Kiel Bay.

A Type IXC U-boat, *U581* was 233 feet long, the same as the Type VIID, the largest version of the previous class which made up the majority of the *Frontboote* in the Atlantic war. However, she had a greater beam, resulting in more internal space and, consequently, a superior cruising range of 13,500 nautical miles. She also had more fire power; *U581* had four torpedo tubes forward and two aft - plus reloads - as well as a 105mm gun on the weather deck and a 37mm *Flakvierling* on the bandstand.

"Ahead standard on both. Steer 045. Ask *Leutnant* Mannstein to come up and relieve me when he's ready," Tröjer ordered. *Leutnant zur See* Wolfgang Mannstein climbed up through the hatch to the bridge. The *Zwei Wache Offizier* or Second Watch Officer, Mannstein was also responsible for communications and gunnery, and had been on duty below in the Control Room.

Tröjer recited, "Steering 045, standard speed on both electric motors, switch to diesels when we reach the centre channel."

"Very good," replied the *Leutnant.*

Tröjer dropped down the hatch straight to the Control Room, using his sea boots on the sides of the ladder to slow his descent. He landed with a *thump* and waited for his eyes to adjust to the gloom. *Obersteursmann* Krüger, the navigating petty officer, was entering their departure time in the log at the navigating position to port. *Zentralemaat* Schultz was manning the main ballast and trim controls.

A U-boat isn't a true submarine, but more of a submersible torpedo-boat - really just a surface vessel that can submerge for short periods to attack or avoid counter attack. To facilitate this, large ballast tanks were filled with seawater to dive or blown empty with compressed air to surface. Additional compensating and trimming tanks were set at strategic spots inside the pressure hull, as well as in the exterior casing, to adjust for any change in the sub's equilibrium.

Forward of Shultz's position were the fore and aft hydroplane controls. Essentially horizontal rudders at the bow and stern which regulated the up and down movement of the boat, the planes were operated by push-button - the large, bolt-like knob on the left for the up angle and the one on the right for the down. In the event of an emergency, the planes could be "switched to hand control" and the thick iron wheels behind used.

Technically, if the U-boat were properly trimmed, the hydroplanes were all that was needed to maintain the ordered depth. *Technically!* In practise, the boat could not be perfectly balanced due to the movement of the crew, stores being used, or torpedoes being fired. As a result, the watch officers were always adjusting the trim and, in the interim, the planes had to be closely monitored.

They weren't manned when the U-boat was on the surface, as the two operators were the bridge lookouts. In the event of a dive, the Control Room petty officer would open the main ballast tanks, starting with the one in the bow, and put the planes to Full Dive. The planesmen would then take their places when they came down from the bridge.

The main steering position at the forward bulkhead, next to the pressure-proof hatch connecting the Control Room to the forward section of the U-boat, was also unoccupied. Another push-button affair, it differed in that there was a gyro-compass repeater above the controls rather than a depth gauge. When on the surface, the boat was steered from a similar arrangement in the Conning Tower above.

All seemed to be in order and Tröjer headed forward to the Captain's cabin. Cubbyhole was more like it! The Captain's quarters were really just part of the main passageway, separated by a heavy curtain which could be drawn, as it was now, for privacy.

Tröjer rapped his knuckles on the bulkhead next to the curtain.

"Enter," came the reply.

Wassermann had been reading his orders. He didn't need to, he'd already read them several times. They were going to Canada, or more exactly, the Strait of Belle Isle, between Newfoundland and Labrador. They were to patrol the area and wait for further orders. *Korvetten-Kapitän* von Bülow, who had seen them off, intimated that German intelligence had an agent who would confirm the presence of shipping in an important anchorage in Newfoundland. The only important anchorage Wassermann could think of was St. John's, the home port of the *Newfoundland Escort Force*. It was defended by shore batteries, torpedo baffles, and an anti-submarine net, and ever since Borcherdt in *U587* had shot two torpedoes at it earlier in the year, the entrance was heavily patrolled by local escort forces. It would be suicide to try to approach St. John's, let alone sink anything. He heard the knock at his door and *Oberleutnant* Tröjer entered.

"We've entered Kiel Bay and are heading towards the Kattegat, *Kapitän*. What are your orders?"

Wassermann stretched. "Tell Krüger to plot a course to Stavanger. We'll top up our fuel there before heading across the Atlantic."

"But, sir," said Tröjer, "we loaded tropical gear. I presumed we were going south."

"Well, you presumed wrongly, *Oberleutnant*. It was a ruse to fool any British spies," replied Wassermann. "We are heading west."

"May I ask where?" enquired Tröjer.

"No, you may not. Now, if there is nothing else to report, you are dismissed, *Leutnant*."

"Very good," Tröjer said stiffly, turned and left.

Wassermann didn't like his *Erster Wache Offizier*. He was handsome, enterprising, very competent, enthusiastic and married. Everything Wassermann was not. Oh, he was once. Well, not married. He'd never married. But he wasn't bad-looking and was once both competent and enthusiastic. His previous captain, *Kapitän-Leutnant* Bartels, under whom he had served as First Watch Officer, had given him quite a good evaluation, which is why he received command of the new *U581* while still an *Oberleutnant.* His current rank and extra half-stripe were a recent development.

However, three years of war had dulled his enthusiasm and, really, the only reason he had joined the *Kriegsmarine* and, in particular, the *U-boat Waffe* in the first place, was family tradition. His late father had commanded a U-boat in the last war.

Oberleutnant Tröjer, on the other hand, did a few patrols early in the war but, due to his exceptional torpedo firing skills, spent a major portion of the past three years instructing at the torpedo school in *Flensburg-Mürwik.* While not an ardent Nazi, First Officer Tröjer was still full of "piss and vinegar," as Wassermann's father would have said, and he didn't like him. Come to think of it, Wassermann didn't much like any of his officers. Mannstein was a great admirer of Tröjer's and a former pupil of his at the torpedo school. Dietrich, the Third Watch Officer, was another young pup full of devotion to *Führer* and Fatherland. *Leutnant zur See* (Ing) Roenneberg, the Engineering Officer, was the oldest man on board, having been promoted upwards through the ranks from the lower deck. He was a dour man and didn't say much but appeared to know what he was doing, judging by their working-up period in the Baltic training flotilla. But Wassermann had not cultivated the normally close relationship between a submarine skipper and his chief engineering officer. Wassermann blamed Roenneberg for that, of course.

Wassermann turned off the lamp and lay back on his bunk. He closed his eyes and let the gentle swaying of the boat and throb of the diesel engines lull him to sleep.

CHAPTER TWO

"WAKE UP, SIR! We're entering St. John's."

Lieutenant Alistair Mitchell, Royal Canadian Naval Reserve (RCNVR), opened his eyes and gratefully accepted a hot cup of cocoa from McDonald, his steward. He'd fallen asleep in his high wooden captain's chair on the open bridge of HMCS Dartmouth. One of the early war-built corvettes, K137 displaced approximately 950 tons, had a 4" gun forward plus a machine gun and depth charges aft - and bounced around like a cork in a good sea. She also had only the most rudimentary navigational and radar equipment, and ASDIC.

ASDIC was the acronym for the Allied Submarine Detection

Investigation Committee, the Anglo-French scientific group that spent twenty years after WWI developing it. Called SONAR by the U.S. Navy, it was basically underwater radar. An emitter attached to the underside of the hull transmitted high-frequency sound impulses - audible pings - that bounced back when they struck an object. The Admiralty in London had declared that it put an end to the U-boat threat.

However, war experience soon revealed its limitations. For one thing, it could only give the range and bearing of the target, not the depth. Nor could it differentiate between a submarine or a whale, or even a large school of fish. The Germans also developed Night Surface Attacks, with devastating effect, which completely negated any advantage of the Asdic.

So all in all, to sink a U-boat, Dartmouth pretty well had to run over it, by accident! But the little corvette, and sixty-eight of her sisters, provided escort services at a time when they were desperately needed.

Mitchell had held command of Dartmouth for over a year. They'd provided escort protection to convoys from Halifax or Sydney, Nova Scotia, to and from New York or the Western Ocean Meeting Point – WESTOMP – the famous Triangle Run, interrupted only by too-short rest periods at St. John's or Halifax. Occasionally, they got some time in New York, always a treat for the crew! This last trip was a fairly typical one: two weeks of stormy weather, sleepless nights, cold food, and the odd moment of stark terror. They'd lost only two ships this time, due mainly to the bad weather rather than the U-boats, which had moved back into the North Atlantic after the American shooting gallery, especially around Newfoundland's east coast. The U-boats had as rough a time as they, and the main objective had been to keep the convoy together and avoid colliding with one another.

"Fort Amherst to port, sir," said Mitchell's Second-in-Command, Lieutenant John Porter, Royal Canadian Naval Volunteer Reserve

(RCNVR). "A sub-lieutenant from 'derry told me torpedoes exploded just below Fort Amherst and Cabot Tower last March. Supposedly, another hit the net but didn't detonate."

"Really?" said Mitchell. The Germans were getting bolder all the time. With the slaughter of merchant ships along the American eastern seaboard that winter and all the other setbacks on land, the Allies might just be losing this war. Things looked pretty bleak.

"They're lowering the net, sir," said Porter. "Hands to Stations for Entering Harbour!" he ordered.

St. John's or Newfyjohn, as all the escort sailors affectionately called the City (they called Halifax Slackers, for good reason), opened up before them. With a natural harbour and the high Southside Hills protecting it from the gales coming off the Atlantic, St. John's had been permanently settled since the 1600s. Newfoundland was the most easterly land mass on the North American continent and 600 miles closer to the convoy routes than

Halifax. As a result, it was a natural choice for an escort base and even the Americans built a large naval/air station in Argentia, Placentia Bay, on Newfoundland's south coast.

Escorts, both Royal Navy (RN) and Royal Canadian Navy (RCN), were berthed three deep along the wharves on the Southside of the harbour. Above them were the long narrow Quonset Huts that housed some of the naval personnel stationed permanently in the City, as well as the crews of the escorts. The rest were housed in the much more comfortable Buckmasters' Field barracks. Officers were usually billeted at the Fort William Officers' Quarters and with the more affluent families of St. John's, although many local residents extended open invitations to all service personnel for Sunday dinner.

"Signal from Captain (D), sir," reported Sub-Lieutenant James Martin, RCNVR, Dartmouth's Signals' Officer, referring to the formal title of the officer in charge of the escorts. "You are to report to Operations immediately upon coming alongside, sir. A car will be waiting."

Great, thought Mitchell as he stirred wearily in his hard wooden chair. All I want is a hot bath, a stiff drink, and 12 hours sleep. However, protocol dictated a visit, so the bath, drink, and sleep, would have to wait.

AN HOUR LATER MITCHELL STOOD before Commander Percival Bloom, Royal Navy, Staff Officer (Operations) for the Newfoundland Escort Force (NEF). "Welcome to St. John's, Lieutenant. Please sit down; you look like hell," Bloom said amiably.

"Thank you, sir," said Mitchell. "It was a rough trip."

"Lose any?"

"Two, sir."

"I guess the worst was the weather."

"Yes, sir."

Bloom folded his hands and looked at Mitchell. "Lieutenant, I'm taking you off ocean escort duties." At Mitchell's alarmed look, he quickly added, "Relax, Lieutenant. You haven't done anything wrong and you're not losing your ship. We have another job for you - a local one based out of here. I'll give you all the details in a week. Dartmouth will be provisioned and re-armed by base personnel and your crew will be given leave. Make sure they all have their Station Cards. In the interim, leave Dartmouth's ship's business to your First Officer, and you take it easy.

You are to be billeted with a Doctor Halley on Topsail Road. A car will take you there. I've met the Doctor; he's a very nice gentleman. And I understand his daughter is quite attractive," Bloom added unnecessarily. He rose, extending his hand to Mitchell. "See you in a week, Lieutenant."

Mitchell, taken aback by the brevity of the interview, also stood and said simply "Thank you, sir," turned and left.

LATER, IN THE BACK SEAT of the staff car, he gazed absently out the window. The driver glanced in the rear-view mirror but said nothing. He'd driven enough escort ship captains to recognize that the young lieutenant didn't want small talk. He left him alone with his thoughts. Mitchell watched as the car passed shop after shop along Water Street, past the Imperial Cafe, which members of the RCN had wrecked in 1941 - not one of the Navy's finer moments. He looked at the people and the streetcars, and was amazed at how similar it all was to Londonderry in Northern Ireland, an earlier appointment as a junior officer. The same style buildings and storefronts, the same streetcars and, being a British crown colony, they even drove on the same side of the road, to the left rather than right of centre, as in Canada and the U.S.

Shortly, they turned into a driveway lined by large trees in full autumn bloom. At the end was a white two-storey house with a wide veranda

across the front and down either side.
Mitchell got out of the car, thanked
the driver, and walked up the five or
six steps to the front door. He was just
about to knock when it opened and a
girl of about twenty stood in front of
him. To Mitchell, she was absolutely
the prettiest girl he had ever seen. She
was slender, with narrow hips and
smallish breasts. Her hair was brown,
her eyes green, and her slightly curved
lips revealed straight white teeth. She
was wearing a simple blue dress with
a small string of pearls at her throat.
Mitchell automatically glanced at her
left hand for an engagement or
wedding ring, and was surprised not
to see one.

"I'm...I'm Lieutenant Mitchell," he
stammered.

"I know," said the girl. "We've been
expecting you. I'm Linda Halley."

Mitchell extended his hand and she
took it, guiding him in through the
doorway at the same time.

"Give me your coat," she said. "Your
bath is running and Dad's in the living
room getting you a brandy."

"You read my mind," said Mitchell, uncertainly.

"Not really," said Linda. "We've had quite a few ships' captains stay here over the past couple of years, and the first things all of them wanted when they got here were a hot bath, a stiff drink, and twelve hours sleep. In that order!" At that, she smiled and said, "And I've fought them all off, Lieutenant." Despite his fatigue, Mitchell also smiled. Not a polite smile, but a genuine pleased smile. He'd been warned! But...he liked this girl already!

"That's better," she said. "You're really quite handsome when you smile. Now, go in and meet Dad. He's right through there." She pointed to a doorway to her right. "I'll let you know when supper and the bath are ready."

Mitchell entered a large, expensively furnished room and immediately saw his host standing by an ornate marble fireplace in which a fire was blazing. One hand held a drink, the other a pipe.

"Lieutenant," he bellowed, "come in, come in. Your drink is on the mantle." Dr. William Halley was a large man - not overweight, just large - and at least six feet tall. He had brown hair, greying at the temples, and looked to Mitchell to be in his mid-fifties. His eyes were green like his daughter's, and his nose prominent and a bit veined. Probably liked his brandy, thought Mitchell.

"Your daughter let me in," Mitchell said hesitantly. "She's very pretty."

"Aye, that she is," said the doctor with a lilt that betrayed his Irish ancestry. Mitchell wondered if he was from Londonderry. Probably not; the Halleys were Catholic, Mitchell remembered from somewhere.

"Don't let that fool you, though, she's as hard as nails," he said, smiling, but added slightly subdued, "like her late mother."

"I'm sorry to hear that, sir," said Mitchell, somewhat uncomfortable.

"Don't be," said the Doctor, brightening. "She had a good life, and enjoyed it to the fullest, like Linda.

She died without regret or suffering, surrounded by her loved ones. I hope to be so lucky."

Just then Linda entered the room and said, "Drink up, Lieutenant. Your bath is ready."

Mitchell drained his brandy and thanked Dr. Halley while being gently led out of the room by Linda Halley. She took him up the large staircase and down the hall to the bathroom. A steaming bath awaited and she showed him the towels and told him his room was next door. He thanked her, somewhat formally, to which she replied, "Don't call me Miss Halley," and left, closing the door behind her. He stripped and slipped into the hot bath. Could anything feel so wonderful, he mused, and immediately stopped as thoughts of Linda Halley came to his mind. He soaked for twenty minutes, then got out of the bath, dried himself, and rinsed out the tub. He found a large, thick, terrycloth bathrobe on a hook on the door and assumed it was for his use. He put it on, picked up his dirty clothes, and padded to the bedroom next door.

The room was dark, except for the soft light given off by a fire in the small marble fireplace. The bed, a large four poster job, had the sheets turned down and next to it on a tray was a cold supper of chicken, ham, coleslaw and potato salad. Next to the tray was an unopened bottle of brandy, a bowl of ice, and a glass. Yes, Mitchell thought, they must have had a lot of escort skippers stay here. He wolfed down supper and had two brandies with a cigarette by the fire. He crawled between the fresh white sheets and fell immediately into a deep, dreamless sleep born of exhaustion, but nurtured by the brandy.

CHAPTER THREE

FRANÇOIS PAQUETTE FLICKED HIS CIGARETTE into the dirty water of Sydney Harbour. Behind him, the bridge watch spoke in quiet voices, this despite the racket of the conveyor emptying the hold of its cargo of iron ore. They'd started this morning and now it was close to suppertime. At the thought, Paquette's stomach growled. Why did I have to stay on watch? he thought. No wireless traffic ever came in while they were unloading.

Captain Jean Garros sauntered over beside Paquette on the bridge wing. "Quiet, eh, François."

"Yes, sir," muttered Paquette.

"We should be finished by eight o'clock. Then we'll move out into the basin and wait for the convoy to form up." Garros looked like the Brittany fisherman he was. He wore a crushed brown fedora and worn leather jacket. Underneath was a woollen turtleneck that was once white but was now a dirty grey. His pants were again wool, and on board he always wore his ratty red flannel slippers. This evening he had a cup of coffee in one hand and the ever-present, foul-smelling *Gauloise* cigarette in the other.

"What time do we depart tomorrow?" asked Paquette, idlely.

"Nine o'clock," said the Captain.

"How many in the convoy?"

"Just three for now," replied Garros. "Ourselves, *Fort Rose,*
and the *Mary P.*"

"The three little pigs," suggested Paquette.

"Cute," chuckled the captain as he returned to the bridge.

Leave tomorrow morning, thought Paquette, cross the Cabot Strait, follow the south coast of Newfoundland and head north along the Southern Shore. Or go through the Strait of Belle Isle and southeast to

Conception Bay. Either way, that should get us to Wabana by Friday, the 31st. I'll send the codeword in the sign-off signal that night.

François Paquette was the wireless operator with the *PBM27*, an acronym for the *Paris-Bordeaux-Marseilles* - the French railway company - in Liverpool when war broke out in '39. After France fell in '40 and the French government moved to Vichy, supposedly independent, Paquette had been approached by a fellow Frenchman in a waterfront bar. He'd heard that François had fascist leanings and German sympathies. How did he know that? Paquette had asked. A friend of yours in Paris, the man replied, Yves Levesque. Paquette once shared a flat with Levesque, who'd been the leader of a fascist cell in Paris during the Spanish Civil War.

Paquette joined the group and attended its meetings and clandestine rallies until he left for Bordeaux to join the *PBM27*. He was not a fanatic, but thought France had grown weak between the wars and admired the

Germans for their recovery from the defeat of

1918, and subsequent chaos, to be the current masters of all Europe. Yes, he was interested. He wanted to be on the winning side and up until the Americans' entry into the war in '41, that was almost assured. He'd agreed to work for the fascist group.

At first it was passing copies of wireless messages to a drop in the bar, but soon he was adding convoy information: sailing times, number of ships and escorts, probable sailing routes, that sort of thing. Then they'd asked him to include codewords in his routine wireless traffic, to let them know when the convoy he was in was leaving port and in what direction. Risky yes, but *PBM27* had her name on her sides in four-foot white letters and Paquette was assured that the U-boats were warned to stay clear.

It seemed to work. Paquette'd been in two Channel convoys that were attacked and escaped unharmed. As a matter of fact, Captain Garros once called him their "lucky package," in reference to his last name. Then they crossed the Atlantic to Canada and started running iron ore from Bell Island, in Newfoundland's Conception Bay, to Sydney, Nova Scotia.

One night in a Sydney waterfront bar, he was approached by another Frenchman who'd asked him if he had "seen any good movies lately?" his old contact phrase, to which he replied, "Not good French ones." The man wanted him to start adding codewords again but this time only when they were anchored at Wabana and there were at least three other ships in company. He again agreed to do so, and last month, as they lay at anchor off Bell Island, he'd added the codeword. The next morning a U-boat slipped in and sank two ships. Once more, the white letters seemed to protect him. Their salvation was actually attributed to another ship, the *Evelyn B*, scaring the U-boat away by wildly firing the ancient gun on her stern. Nevertheless, things were getting a bit close to home. He knew a couple of the guys killed on board the

Saganaga. Paquette was beginning to wonder if the Nazi cause was still the same as his.

"Mister Paquette."

François turned to see Oliver Bligh, their English First Mate, framed in the doorway. The men called him Captain Bligh, of *Mutiny on the Bounty* fame. "Yes, sir," he replied.

"You may go below for supper. I'll notify you if there is any wireless traffic," he said formally. Always proper.

"Yes, sir. Thank you, sir" said Paquette, with just a trace of sarcasm, as he exited the bridge and went down the stairs to the mess. The aroma of fresh bread met him at the door and he saw Banh Chan (nicknamed Ban-Ban), their baker, lay out hot buns. He smiled when he saw Paquette.

"François, Papa Henri has just made some soup to go with these buns," he said, inclining his head towards the cook.

It was funny to hear French coming from an Oriental, but Chan was from French Indochina and spoke it fluently. Paquette took two buns and grabbed a bowl from the rack, sliding it along the counter until he was across from Papa Henri. He didn't know Papa's last name, he had always been just "Papa Henri."

"'allo, François," said Papa with his peculiar Marseilles accent. He was a big man with the face of a boxer, his nose broken several times in barroom brawls all over the world. He was a good cook, though, and a fine enough shipmate, but you didn't go out drinking with him in port, not if you wanted to stay out of trouble.

"'allo, Papa," said Paquette, "some soup, *s'il vous plait.*" Papa smiled as he poured out a healthy portion of soup and winked at Paquette, Frenchman to Frenchman. The radioman thanked the cook, and nodded to Ban-Ban, as he took his soup and buns, and found a spot at the end of one of the long mess tables. Across from him sat Tassill n'Ager, an Algerian, and next to him, Jean Bourgeois, a French-Canadian from Montreal.

"No traffic?" said n'Ager.

"None."

"Did the Captain say when we were leaving?" asked Bourgeois.

"Tomorrow morning," answered Paquette with a mouthful of bun. He swallowed and continued. "Around nine o'clock."

"That'll get us into Wabana Friday afternoon."

"I guess so," said Paquette. "Why?"

"Oh, just curious," replied the Canadian.

"Remember what that did to the cat," interjected n'Ager with a peculiar smile. Of course, n'Ager always had a peculiar smile. It made Paquette uneasy

Paquette continued eating, bored with the conversation as n'Ager and Bourgeois exchanged barbs. While he liked his messmates, overall, sometimes they got on his nerves. Yes, he remembered what curiosity did to the cat, he thought as he finished his supper, put the dirty bowl on the counter, and left the mess. But, he felt

guiltily, best to leave curiosity behind,
nowadays

CHAPTER FOUR

FIRST OFFICER TRÖJER WIPED THE LENSES of his *Zeiss* binoculars for the hundredth time. Bad weather had hit them a day out of Norway and followed them all the way across the Atlantic. Many of the crew were seasick, and added to the normal U-boat stink of damp, mould, body odour, and diesel exhaust, was the sour-sweet stench of vomit.

It had been rough going and *Kapitän-Leutnant* Wassermann spent most of it in his cabin. Only the occasional brief, awkward meal in the wardroom, or quick visit to the Control Room to check their progress, had interrupted his self-imposed exile. He still hadn't relayed their operational orders to Tröjer except that they were heading to the east coast of Canada via a roundabout route south of Greenland.

Relations continued to deteriorate between the Captain and the rest of his officers. Morale amongst the crew was also poor, and the weather and conditions on board the U-boat didn't improve things. There'd been a few altercations in the fore-ends that Troger'd had to deal with. About the only bright spot was the news that Tröjer's wife, Ingrid, had given birth to a baby boy at her parent's house in Krefeld, near Hannover. He was named, by previous agreement, Kurt, after Tröjer's father. Even then, a perfect opportunity for morale-boosting, the Captain allowed only the officers to share a couple of bottles of champagne. The rest of the crew were excluded.

"TARGET GREEN 45," YELLED FEISER, the starboard lookout, over the howling of the wind.

Tröjer trained his binoculars on the bearing and sighted a fast-moving target about three miles distant. Too fast for a merchantman, must be a warship or possibly a troop transport, he thought. The British were using their large ocean liners for troop carriers, allowing them to sail independently, relying on their superior speed to keep them safe from U-boat attack.

"Action Stations," yelled Tröjer down the voicepipe. "Steer 320," putting *U581* on an intercept course. He added, "And call the *Kaleu*."

Forward, in the *Bugtorpedoraum* at the bow, all tubes were flooded and the bow caps opened. The ejection system was fully charged with compressed air, to fire the torpedoes, and the petty officer in charge stood by the manual firing keys - just in case the ones in

the Control Room failed. The seven-meter-long missiles, coated in a layer of grease, and capable of speeds up to 44 knots, lay ready and waiting for action.

Wassermann appeared on the bridge, dressed in Sou'wester, with a pair of binoculars around his neck.

"Fast target, possibly a transport, bearing 315, sir," said Tröjer without preamble. Wassermann raised his binoculars in the direction indicated by Tröjer. He stared a long time, too long for Tröjer, who volunteered, "I've ordered Action Stations, sir. All forward torpedoes are ready."

Wassermann didn't answer but leaned over the voicepipe and ordered, "Stand down from Action Stations and resume original course and speed." Tröjer stood open-mouthed, staring at Wassermann. The U-boat captain turned to him and said, "Too fast, Number One. We would waste time and fuel chasing it to no avail."

"But sir, we should at least try."

"No, *Oberleutnant*, we should follow our orders."

"Our orders are to sink enemy ships, *sir*," said Tröjer angrily, "not run from them!"

"That's enough, *Oberleutnant*!" Wassermann paused and looked directly at Tröjer. "Or would you like me to relieve you of duty?"

Tröjer turned without answering, and raised his binoculars to his eyes as the U-boat heeled over slightly to its previous course. Wassermann stared at Tröjer's back for a moment, then went below without comment. Luft and Feiser, the two lookouts, exchanged glances with Capito, the Chief Petty Officer of the Watch, who glared back, and then resumed their vigil. In his own mind, Capito, too, wondered about the *Kaleu*.

Another wave washed over the bow and crashed against the front of the Conning Tower. The *U581* continued its lonely voyage west.

CHAPTER FIVE

THE FORCE *W* CANADIAN ARMY HEADQUARTERS were located at the corner of Rennies Mill Road and Circular Road. Leaves swirled about their feet as Alistair Mitchell and Linda Halley walked past it, arm in arm, along Circular Road. Linda shivered slightly as they paused to look at *Canada House*, the residence of the Canadian High Commissioner, with its high, wrought-iron fence and manicured grounds. Mitchell put his arm around her and they continued on their way. He was completely, hopelessly, in love with Linda Halley. It had started slowly. The morning after he'd arrived, he had walked into the kitchen looking for a cup of tea and saw Linda sitting at the table talking to Mrs. O'Brien, the housekeeper. "Good morning, sunshine," she said. "Sleep well?"

"Yes, thank you," he replied.

"Like some tea?" she said, getting up. "Have a seat, I'll get you a cuppa."

He sat and as he drank his tea and smoked a cigarette, she asked him about himself. Normally a shy, quiet man, Mitchell found it easy to open up to her. He told her he was from Prince Edward Island and his father was a fisherman.

"I thought all they did on PEI was grow potatoes," she said with a smile.

"I thought all they did in Newfoundland was fish," he returned.

"That's about it. That and sealing, although the war stopped the latter. How long have you been in the Navy?"

"I've been in the Reserve for a number of years, and was called up when war was declared. I've been at it ever since. Seems like a hundred years."

"How old are you anyway, Lieutenant?" inquired Linda.

"Now who's being formal? My name is Alistair, but call me Mitch. I'm twenty-four, or will be in December."

"Alistair," she stated." Aren't you awfully young to captain a ship?"

"Not really. My Second-in-Command is twenty-two. Blandford, my gunnery officer, just turned twenty-one, and Martin, my third officer, is only nineteen. It's a young man's war."

That night they'd gone to a dance at the *Bella Vista Country Club* on Torbay Road. Despite being asked by several officers, including Lieutenant Porter, she chose to dance only with Mitchell. She fit perfectly in his arms and was an excellent dancer. "Mrs. Fagan's dancing classes," she confessed. It didn't matter to Mitchell, he just enjoyed having her with him. That night, after they'd gotten home, she kissed him lightly on the cheek at his bedroom door and told him she'd had a wonderful time. He found it hard to get to sleep, his mind filled with thoughts of Linda Halley, and his feelings towards her. Probably just being a good hostess, he decided.

But, no. The next day, they had gone for a walk and she slipped her hand in his and said, "I like you, Lieutenant Alistair Mitchell." He usually hated being called *Alistair*, but didn't mind it when she did.

The week flew by, the days filled with long, leisurely walks to Bowering Park or shorter ones along Water Street to nearby Victoria Park. The nights, they spent at the *Nickel Theatre*, the *Newfoundland Hotel Dining Room*, or the *Crow's Nest*. The *Seagoing Officers Club* was located in a loft next to the War Memorial, between Water Street and Duckworth Street, and had been founded earlier in the year by Captain (D), E.R. Mainguy. It was the favourite watering hole of the officers of the *Newfoundland Escort Force* and the walls were adorned with the unofficial crests of all the ships in the Command. Being a new addition, Dartmouth had yet to be so honoured, although Lieutenant Porter was working on it.

But Mitchell was due to report to Commander Bloom first-thing in the morning. Despite being intrigued by the prospect of a new assignment, he didn't want to be separated from Linda. Well, he thought, Bloom did say he would be based out of St. John's.

They stopped at a graveyard and Linda asked to go in. "I like looking at all the old headstones," she said. "Besides, it'll take us back to the house." They followed the path until they came to a newer monument. "Mom," was all she said and started to quietly cry. He gathered her into his arms and held her close until the tears subsided. She looked up at him, and he bent down and gently kissed her upturned mouth. "Linda...'" he started.

"I love you too," she said quietly and took his hand. They walked in silence the rest of the way home and had a small supper in the kitchen. That night she again kissed him at his door and said, "Good night."

"Would you like to come in?"

The words were out of his mouth before he could stop them. Realizing the magnitude of his proposal, Mitchell stammered, "I'm, I'm, Linda, I'm so sorry . . ."

Linda took his hands in hers and looked into his eyes. Hers glistened and a small tear rolled down her cheek. "I can't," she whispered. She turned and rushed into her room across the hall. Mitchell swore at himself and entered his own room, closing the door behind him.

Linda slipped off her dress and pulled on her flannel nightgown; it was October, after all. She sat in front of the mirror and brushed her hair, her mind in turmoil. She had wanted to say yes. Her heart wanted her to say yes. The woman in her wanted to say yes. She longed for his touch, his caress. But twenty years of Catholic upbringing wouldn't let her. Oh, she wasn't one of those Bible-kissing, Holy Picture, Blessed Virgin types. Well, maybe a little. She was a virgin, and she'd resisted all the other terribly handsome young naval officers, sometimes strenuously, that had stayed with the Halley's over the past few years. But she'd never been in love before, not really in love. Alistair Mitchell was different. Special! She would die for Alistair Mitchell! So, why wouldn't she go to bed with him? Goddamn the Ascension Sisters!!!!

Linda finished brushing her hair, climbed into bed and turned off the lamp. She stared into the darkness - adjusted her pillow - she tried to get more comfortable. However, sleep would not come.

CHAPTER SIX

"YOU MAY GO IN NOW, Lieutenant."

Mitchell stood before Commander Bloom's desk, hat under his arm.

"Sit down, Lieutenant. My word, you look a hundred times better than the last time I saw you," said the Commander. "The Halleys must have treated you very well."

"Yes, sir, thank you. They were very kind."

"How is your ship?"

"Lieutenant Porter reports her fully fuelled and armed, and all crew on board," Mitchell replied.

"Good," responded Bloom. "Now, your assignment..." Bloom shuffled through some papers on his desk, then looked up at Mitchell. "Last

September, a U-boat sailed into Wabana in Conception Bay, just west of here, and sank two ore carriers, pretty as you please. She broke surface briefly after she sank one of the ships and the shore batteries opened fire, and even one of the other ships let off a few rounds, but near as we can tell, the U-boat got away scot-free. A survivor from the *Lord Strathcona* indicated that they may have inadvertently rammed the submarine just before it sank them, but no oil or wreckage was found. The best we could hope for is a bit of superstructure damage.

"As you can imagine, the Commodore hit the roof! The locals, of course, are blaming it on us. Dereliction of duty, they're saying. FONF has ordered a continual patrol of the entrance to Conception Bay, as well as inshore patrols by Fairmiles from Harbour Grace. *Dartmouth* has been assigned the patrol of the entrance.

"There's a convoy of ore carriers on their way here now, and you will relieve the escorting corvette, HMCS *Chedabucto*, off St. John's, and continue to Wabana anchorage with the convoy. You're to patrol the entrance to Conception Bay until you are relieved by *Chedabucto*, four days from now, at which point you'll escort the ore carriers to Sydney. Any questions, Lieutenant?" Bloom finished.

"Sir, *Dartmouth* has only the most basic Asdic equipment, which won't be much good in shallow water. A U-boat could go underneath us and we might not detect her. If she goes in on the surface, our radar won't be able to tell the difference between a target and the wavetops, especially against the cliffs closer to shore," Mitchell explained.

"I know, Lieutenant," said Bloom patiently, "but it'll have to do. Hopefully, any adventurous U-boat skipper will be discouraged by a patrolling warship in the vicinity."

"Yes, sir," said Mitchell, unconvinced. "When do we rendezvous with the convoy?"

"1200 hours," replied Bloom, "just outside the Narrows," referring to the entrance to St. John's Harbour. Bloom stood up, as did Mitchell, and extended his hand. Mitchell shook it. "Good luck, Lieutenant," said Bloom.

Mitchell said, "Thank you, sir," and left.

Commander Bloom watched him leave and let out a small sigh. What he hadn't told Mitchell was that Intelligence suspected a spy, either on Bell Island or on board one of the ore carriers. U-boat traffic had been picked up further north and it wouldn't take one any more than a day to reach Conception Bay once given the word that targets were there. Telling the young lieutenant wouldn't have made much difference, Bloom figured. Just confuse the issue, really. He sat down, took off his glasses and rubbed the bridge of his nose. He put his glasses back on, picked up a sheet of correspondence and began to read some more bad news. I hope you're ready, Lieutenant Mitchell, thought Bloom.

MITCHELL   RETURNED
LIEUTENANT PORTER'S SALUTE
as he stepped off the prow onto the
deck of HMCS *Dartmouth*. "Welcome
back, sir," said Porter.

"Thank you, John. I'll brief you on
our orders in my cabin, when you're
ready."

"Yes, sir. I'll get Bob to get us under
way," said Porter, referring to
Lieutenant Robert Blandford RCNVR,
the second officer.

"I'll take her out when we're ready.
Let me know when we're all set," said
Mitchell, and headed aft along the
deck to his cabin. Porter climbed to
the bridge and gave orders to get the
ship underway. Lines were drawn in
and the water around Dartmouth's
stern started to boil as the single
screw bit into it. Slowly, she parted
from the wharf and headed out into
the chop of the harbour.

Porter handed the ship over to
Blandford with the statement, "I'll be
with the Captain. Let me know when

we're approaching the net," and exited the rear of the open bridge. As he headed down the midships passageway, he constantly had to weave around other members of the crew preparing *Dartmouth* for sea. Everything had to be securely fastened down; in heavy weather a loose fire extinguisher could become a dangerous projectile. He paused by the radio shack and poked his head in, saying, "Anything new, Peters?"

"No, sir," replied the operator, still adjusting the dials.

Porter continued on his way, stopping occasionally to give a direction or acknowledge a greeting. Despite being constantly at sea over the past thirteen months, *Dartmouth* was a happy ship. Oh, there were the usual grumblers, there always were, but overall they had a tight, efficient crew; at least, as much as they could be with what they had. *Dartmouth*'s equipment was obsolescent when she slid down the ways in 1941 and despite some upgrading in Charleston, South Carolina, mainly enlarging the bridge to accommodate the relocated steering position, she desperately needed modern gear. The British escorts always seemed to have the latest improvements, and what irked Porter the most was that the Brit's seemed to always get it first. We're supposed to be Allies, remember?

He reached the Captain's Sea Cabin and knocked on the door. Without waiting for a reply, he opened it and went in.

"Oh, hi, John," said Mitchell. "Come on in."

"Boy, Mitch, she must be something. I haven't seen you look this good in a long time."

"Yes, she is, rather."

"Is it serious?"

"Uh-huh."

"Her, too?"

"I think so"

"Good. Should I start polishing my sword for the wedding?" Porter smiled.

"That could be a little premature," laughed Mitchell, "but you might want to dig it out." Turning serious, he said," Now, to the mission at hand."

He put a cigarette in his mouth and offered the pack to Porter, who took one, then lit both with his lighter. Mitchell reviewed everything Commander Bloom had told him and, with the aid of a chart of the area on his bunk, he showed Porter his patrol plan.

"The two Fairmiles will be inshore, close to the anchorage, to give immediate support if anything happens," he said. "We'll stay out here, close enough to respond if need be but also in a position to intercept anything trying to penetrate the Bay."

"John," said Mitchell, looking straight at Porter, "we've got to be really on the ball this time. With the gear we've got, a U-boat will have to do something stupid for us to detect her before she attacks. Make sure we're ready if she does."

"Count on it," said Porter seriously.

"Good," said Mitchell, glancing at his watch. "We should be rendezvousing with the convoy in about twenty minutes. Give me a moment and I'll join you on the bridge." Porter stood up, extinguished his cigarette in the ashtray on the small desk in the corner and left. Mitchell stared at the chart a minute, then folded it up and put it under his arm. He looked around the cabin to see if he had forgotten anything, then opened the door and went out into the confusion of the passageway. The space was silent, and through the scuttle above the desk, the rough, rocky cliffs and the concrete bunkers of Fort Amherst glided by.

CHAPTER SEVEN

THE MESSAGE ENDED and François Paquette acknowledged receipt and signed off. He got up from his chair in the Marconi room on top of the superstructure and headed forward to the bridge. "Captain," he said when he got there, "message from St. John's. Our escort relief has left port and will meet us off Freshwater Bay at 1200. We are to maintain course and speed during the changeover."

"Bon," said Garros, "thank you, François." He looked at the chronometer on the bulkhead forward. "We should see her shortly."

Sure enough, in the distance to port, HMCS *Dartmouth* came into view. She was ploughing through the 10 foot seas, throwing up a large bow wave as she burst from one crest to another. The wind was coming from the northeast at about thirty knots and the little warship was having a tough time of it. As she approached the convoy, blinker signals were exchanged with *Chedabucto*, who shortly detached with a final, "Leaving the office." *Dartmouth* took her station to seaward.

The convoy maintained its spearhead formation with the *PBM27* in the van, then *Fort Rose* and the *Mary P*, followed by *Spring Valley* and the Greek *Pilos*, which had joined them from Halifax. The two Fairmiles trailed. Following an Admiralty-approved zigzag pattern, they continued north at a steady eight knots for the next four hours. They passed Torbay and Pouch Cove, finally rounding Cape St. Francis and heading south into Conception Bay. The convoy kept to the deep water channel, altering only when entering the sheltered anchorage between Bell Island and Portugal Cove on the mainland. The Dominion and Scotia Piers, with their long conveyor belts reaching the water's edge, were empty, awaiting the arrival of the convoy. *PBM27* and *Fort Rose* immediately docked and shortly iron ore started to fill their holds.

The other three ships cut their engines and anchored, still in formation. *Dartmouth* and one of the two Fairmiles continued through the anchorage, leaving *Q075*. The second Fairmile, *Q087*, detached to patrol the southern passage as *Dartmouth* rounded Bell Island and headed for the mouth of Conception Bay. The wind had dropped and, at twelve knots, she made good progress. Mitchell started his patrol pattern, a kind of elongated figure-eight, across the entrance, each leg taking approximately 30 minutes at a speed calculated to give the best Asdic conditions. He returned to his cabin after the first pattern and McDonald brought him supper. After eating, he sat at his desk for awhile, smoking a cigarette and finishing his tea, his thoughts on Linda Halley. With a slight shake, he brought himself out of his reverie and, gulping down the last of the tea - now cold - he put on his duffle coat and left the cabin for the bridge.

FRANÇOIS PAQUETTE HAD ALSO FINISHED HIS SUPPER and sat before the radio in the Marconi Room at the top of *PBM27*s superstructure, smoking a cigarette and drinking coffee. The ship was quiet with most of the crew ashore and only himself, Bligh, Able Seaman Valentine, Ban-Ban, and Second Engineer Denis on board. Paquette thought about how he was going to slip the codeword into his last transmission of the night. Actually, the system was almost foolproof, due mainly to its simplicity. All Paquette had to do was include a word in the message; either 'sleep', signalling the anchorage as being full, or 'awake', for it being empty. Radio operators, particularly civilian ones, were notorious for their on-air chatter and many prided themselves on their eloquence, quoting Shakespeare, Oscar Wilde, or some other notable, especially American movie stars. Rhett Butler's "Frankly, my dear, I don't give a damn" was particularly popular. It drove the military types crazy and, of course, that made it all the more fun.

But, Paquette had started to doubt, over the last little while, whether he really was doing the right thing. From what he'd read of the Nazi *Blitzkrieg* through Western Europe, and now their campaign in the Soviet Union, the *Wehrmacht* was more of a conquering army than a liberating one. And he had heard disquieting rumours over the past little while about massacres and death camps. Uncertain, Paquette decided on a quote and lit another cigarette, waiting impatiently for eleven o'clock.

To distract himself, Paquette decided to run down to the mess and get a cup of coffee to pass the time. He got out of his chair and headed out of the Marconi Room, figuring he had enough time to get below and back before he had to send his message. He entered the mess, and Ban-Ban noticed him right away and smiled. He came over to the counter, at the same time filling up a coffee cup for Paquette. "Hey, my friend," said the Asian. "No traffic on the radio tonight?"

"No," replied the Frenchman, "It's usually pretty quiet this time of night. How are you?"

"Ah, I am fine, I guess. Just got a letter from my wife. She's in Saigon with her mother. I haven't heard from her in a year."

"Oh, yeah," replied Paquette, "how is she doing?"

"Not too well, I'm afraid" answered the baker. "The Japs are barbarians. They've kidnapped thousands of women to be *comfort girls* – whores! - for their troops. She is very afraid. I wish I'd stayed. I don't know what I could do about it, but at least she wouldn't be so scared. We were trying to have a baby when I left." The little

Asian lowered his eyes, and Paquette felt his fear.

"I'm so sorry, Ban-Ban. Is there anything I can do?"

The man looked up at him, and replied, wearily, "Is there anything anyone can do?"

Paquette didn't have an answer to that, and just mumbled his thanks to the baker and headed back to the wireless office.

FINALLY, THE TIME CAME and Paquette banged out his message:

PBM27 AT POINT BAKER ITEM DOG PETER (Bell Island Dominion Pier) SIGNING OFF. AND NOW I LAY ME DOWN TO SLEEP. 01/11/42.

St. John's acknowledged receipt of the signal. Paquette turned off the radio, got up and stretched. It was all too easy, he thought as he closed the door and headed for the bridge to report to Bligh before he went to bed.

THREE HUNDRED MILES out in the Atlantic, the *U502* also received the transmission. On the way to her patrol area, Admiral Karl Dönitz, the *Befehlshaber-der-U-boote* (Commander-in-Chief of U-boats), ordered her to take station west of the Flemish Cap on the Newfoundland Grand Banks for weather reports and wireless surveillance. *U502*'s wireless operator, *Oberfunkmeister* Clausen, included the message with his own of the weather conditions and sent it to U-boat headquarters in Kerneval, outside Lorient on the Normandy coast. It was early morning in France but the signal was sent directly to the Admiral, who was still in the Situation Room. He read the brief note and in clipped German gave instructions to the waiting sailor, who saluted, turned, and left.

Dönitz walked over to the large table with a map of the North Atlantic, from Britain in the east to Canada in the west, on its smooth surface. The map was divided into squares, which were again divided into smaller squares, each with its own alphanumeric designation. He picked up a small wooden model of a U-boat labelled *U581* and moved it from the coast of Labrador down to square BB63 - Conception Bay. He turned to his Chief of Operations, *Kapitän zur See* Eberhard Gödt, and smiling, rubbed his hands together.

CHAPTER EIGHT

FUNKMAAT GUNTHER KLEIN OPENED HIS EYES, suddenly alert as he heard *U581*'s call sign come in over the speaker above his head. He quickly grabbed a pencil and started to write on the yellow paper pad in front of him.

U581 had been on station off the coast of Labrador for a week and, other than a small sailing ship not worth a torpedo, they'd had no sightings at all. They spent the day submerged to avoid aircraft patrols and surfaced at nightfall to ventilate the boat and charge the batteries. The monotony was getting to everyone, and there had been a few more arguments in the cramped fore-ends where the majority of the crew lived and worked.

Their daylong dives meant boring hours of inactivity with the air getting almost unbreathable towards the end. It was usually only when they surfaced at night that most of the work was done. Torpedoes were routined, meals cooked, and garbage thrown overboard in sacks weighed down with crushed cans and broken tools, or anything else that would help them sink. The heads were used, and cigarettes lit, and generally the mood of the crew improved.

What they needed, though, were targets, something worth firing a torpedo at. That would give the men more room up forward and lift everyone's spirits. But the sea was barren. They were not alone in that, of course. They'd exchanged signals with both Eric Topp's *Red Devil Boat U522*, and Schäfer*'s U509* who was also on his first war patrol and a flotilla mate. Both were further south, in the Gulf of St. Lawrence, and neither'd had much luck, although *U509* claimed some small successes.

Klein finished writing and tapped out an acknowledgement on the key. He decoded it using the Top Secret *Schüsselmaschine M*, tore off the top sheet of the pad when he'd finished, and headed across the passageway to the Captain's cabin, just aft of the wardroom. He knocked on the bulkhead, next to the drawn curtain, and called, "*Kaleu*, message from U-boat Command." He heard a muffled *Komm* and drew across the curtain. Wassermann was just swinging into a sitting position on his bed, having been napping. He took the message from Klein and read it.

"Get the First Officer, please," he said, standing up.

Tröjer was in the *Offizierraum*, next door, having supper when he heard the signal come in and was waiting for the Captain's summons. He pushed past Klein, and Wassermann handed him the sheet. Wassermann nodded to Klein, who returned to his station, and drew the curtain back across the doorway. Tröjer read:

IN THE ORE-LOADING HARBOUR OF ST. JOHN'S, NEWFOUNDLAND, GRID SQUARE BB-63.

THERE ARE PROBABLY STEAMSHIPS. FAVOURABLE POSSIBILITIES TO ATTACK. ENDEAVOUR TO FORCE YOUR WAY INTO THE HARBOUR. AVOID PBM27.

He looked up at Wassermann who was spreading a chart out on his bunk. Like the Admiral's table in France, it was divided into squares, further subdivided into smaller squares. With Tröjer looking over his shoulder, Wassermann found the grid labelled BB, and with his forefinger, pointed to square 63. Together, both men muttered, "Conception Bay."

Tröjer said, "You were expecting this signal, weren't you, Captain?" At Wassermann's nod he continued, "That's why you wouldn't waste fuel chasing that target last week." Again

Wassermann nodded. "Why didn't you tell me?"

"Because technically, I didn't know," Wassermann answered.

"I don't understand."

"Before we left Kiel, *Korvetten-Kapitän* von Bülow told me, in confidence, that the *Abwehr* had an agent who was confirming shipping in an important anchorage in Newfoundland. I didn't know where or when. I was even afraid it would be St. John's. I'd forgotten about Wabana at Bell Island; I heard that Rüggeberg in *U513* had some luck there back in September."

"And the AVOID PBM27?" questioned Tröjer.

"I'm assuming it's a ship, maybe the one the agent is on. If it is, I don't know how we're supposed to identify it. They don't exactly have their names in big white letters on their sides!"

"Some of the French ones do," said Tröjer.

"You're joking! Really?" said Wassermann, surprised.

"Some of the larger fleets; the company initials and a number," answered Tröjer, then added, "Why couldn't you tell me all this before now?"

"Because, if anything happened to us, if we were sunk and prisoners taken, I would be the only one who knew about the agent. And I would go down with *U581*," Wassermann concluded.

"I see," said Tröjer with grudgingly new respect for his Captain. "When do we go?"

"Now," said Wassermann, pulling back the curtain and going out into the passageway, heading for the *Zentrale*. He reached the open, oval-shaped pressure-tight hatch and ducked into the central compartment. Word had spread through the boat, and there were more than the usual number of crew present. *Leutnant* Dietrich was already at the small chart table, and Wassermann and Tröjer shouldered in next to him. He winked at Tröjer behind the Captain's back, but Tröjer ignored him.

Wassermann took the dividers and measured the most direct route to Conception Bay. He turned and said to the helmsman, "*Steuermann,* change course to 135, maximum speed!"

"Aye, aye, *Kaleu,*" came the reply. The sailor reached up and slid the engine room telegraphs to *Full.* In the next compartment astern, the chime of the telegraph repeater attracted the attention of *Dieselmaat* Hirschfeld, who opened up the throttles on the two massive 9-cylinder MAN diesel engines.

Wassermann turned to Tröjer. "Tell *Leutnant* Roenneberg to get every knot he can out of the engines, Number One. I want to be as close as possible before we have to dive at dawn. We need to be at Conception Bay by tomorrow afternoon. Understood?"

"Absolutely, *Kaleu,*" said Tröjer with a smile.

"Very good, *Oberleutnant,*" said Wassermann, once again the aloof commanding officer. But now the men looked at him in a new light. This was a fighting captain -their captain. Wassermann left the Control Room to return to his cabin while Tröjer headed aft to the engine room to talk to Roenneberg. Dietrich grinned widely at the crew in the Control Room and clapped his hands. Action at last!

CHAPTER NINE

THE NORTHEAST WIND formed cats'-paws on the steel grey waves as it blew across the mouth of Conception Bay. Mitchell opened his eyes and started rubbing his arms to warm himself. He must have fallen asleep.

"Morning, Sub. What time is it?"

"Good morning, Captain," replied Sub-Lieutenant Martin. "0630, sir."

"Sun will be up shortly," said Mitchell.

"Yes, sir. Would you like some cocoa?"

"No thanks, Sub. I'm going below to have breakfast. Is McDonald up yet, do you know?" enquired Mitchell.

"I think so, sir."

"Good. I'll be in my cabin if you need me, Sub."

"Yes, sir."

Mitchell got up and headed aft. He met McDonald along the way, a tray of mugs in his hands, and asked for breakfast. McDonald replied, "In your cabin, sir," and continued on his way to the bridge. The man's telepathic, thought Mitchell, as he opened the door to his cabin and saw his breakfast on the desk, steam rising from the cup of tea. Mitchell had just taken off his duffle coat and sat down when there was a knock on his door. Now what? he thought, but called instead, "Come in!"

Peters, the wireless operator, poked his head around the door. "Sorry to bother you, sir. R/T from *Q087*. All quiet at the anchorage; *PBM27* and *Fort Rose* loaded and anchored mid-harbour. *Mary P* and *Spring Valley* now loading, the *Pilos* to follow."

"Very good. Thank you, Peters," said Mitchell. Peters nodded and left, closing the door quietly behind him. The *Mary P*'s only small, thought Mitchell, she'll be loaded in a couple of hours. That will leave just *Spring*

Valley and *Pilos* at dockside overnight. We'll be able to leave tomorrow lunchtime and reach Sydney the next day. Let's hope tonight's quiet also. With that, he put it all out of his mind and concentrated on more pleasant thoughts - Linda Halley.

He was going to ask her to marry him, after he received permission from Dr. Halley, of course. But would she say yes? The war was far from over and a navy lieutenant didn't make much money. She probably wouldn't want to leave her father just yet anyway, so he didn't need to worry about renting a flat. Not that there were many around to rent.

And she had a job, he thought, although he couldn't quite remember what it was she said she did. He had a vague idea that she was in one of the women's volunteer forces – the Wrens, WACS, WAFS??? He really should have paid attention. And would she want kids? He did, a whole boodle of them. Would they move to PEI after the war or stay in Newfoundland? What would he do after the war? Go back to school, probably. But how would he support Linda and the kids if he did that? Hold on, he told himself. I haven't even asked her yet. She might say no. God, he hoped not!

Mitchell finished his breakfast, slid back his chair and put his feet up on the bunk. He took a cigarette from the pack on his desk and lit it. Reaching for his tea, he took a sip and stared idly out the scuttle. It was full daylight now and looked like it would be fairly pleasant. Not much chance of an attack during the day, he thought, but they'd better stay alert, just in case. A U-boat might now be reconnoitring the Bay. With that, he picked up the inter-ship handset on the bulkhead next to him and dialled the bridge. Martin answered, and Mitchell asked him to assign extra ratings with binoculars to keep a sharp lookout to seaward for a periscope. That done, he extinguished his cigarette, drank the last of his tea and lay down on his bunk. He thought again of Linda Halley but was soon asleep.

FIFTY MILES NORTHWEST, another ship's captain was also drifting off to sleep. They dived at dawn, but Wassermann had been up most of the night studying the chart and planning his strategy. He decided they would go in on the surface, but defences in place at Bell Island would determine when and where. Chances were that there was at least one patrol boat, probably more, as well as guns and spotlights at the anchorage. He'd make his final plans after they reached their destination, in about nine hours. Until then he'd better get some sleep. It could be a very busy night.

CHAPTER TEN

U502 DUG HER BOWS into the wave and made a sickening corkscrew motion that lifted her propellers out of the water. She reached the crest, slid down the trough and hit the next breaker. The bridge watch held on, even though each was tethered by steel cable to the Conning Tower fairing. Many a U-boatman had been injured skidding along water-slick grating, breaking a leg or suffering a concussion on one of the numerous protrusions.

All were wet and cold. Nothing could stop the frigid waters of the North Atlantic from seeping in around collars and armholes, no matter how tight and supposedly waterproof the heavy-weather clothing. The northeast wind cut through the rubber coats and hoods, and made exposed skin pink and raw looking.

Down below, conditions weren't much better. Condensation dripped off the overheads and the erratic motion of the U-boat sent food flying to the deck. In the fore-ends, one always moved with a hand clutching the torpedo rail for fear of being thrown across the compartment into the unyielding steel of the pressure hull. The smell of vomit prevailed, as those with the weaker stomachs lay in their bunks, sure they were dying and afraid they wouldn't.

Oberfunkmeister Ruprecht Clausen, a veteran of the Atlantic war and, consequently, not as prone to seasickness as some of his less seasoned *Kameraden*, smoked a cigarette and sipped a cup of coffee. His position as Senior Radio Operator excluded him from watchkeeping duties on the bridge and he spent his time in the radio room, next to the forward Control Room hatch. He looked up as *Leutnant* Adolf

Limbrünner, the Second Watch
Officer, entered with a coded message.
"Another weather report, sir?"

"Yes," replied Limbrünner.

"What a wasted effort. It's been
lousy for the past week and probably
will be for the next!"

"I know," answered Limbrünner.
"Hopefully we'll get some orders soon."
The U-boat gave another sudden lurch
and the *Leutnant* made a quick grab
for the doorframe. "I don't know if I
can stand much more of this!"

U502 had been on station west of
the Flemish Cap for the past week,
passing weather reports and any
enemy transmissions they picked up.
It was boring, miserable duty, and the
U-boat's crew hated it. After all, the
German U-boat, the most capable and
deadly submarine in the world, was
designed to sink enemy ships, not act
as a bloody weather station. Clausen
accepted the signal from *Leutnant*
Limbrünner and started to send it out
over the airwaves.

Above, *Oberleutnant* Luft, the
Erster Wache Offizier, wiped the

lenses of his powerful *Zeiss* binoculars. It was a useless action. He couldn't see anything through the spray and rain anyway. Neither could any of them hear above the howling of the wind and crashing

of the waves against the Conning Tower. As a result, nobody saw or heard the aircraft approaching from the southwest. The first they knew of it was when the RCAF PBY *Canso* flying boat roared overhead, depositing a 450 pound depthbomb on either side of the submarine. The explosions sent a 75-foot plume into the air and Flying Officer Collins saw the U-boat dive into the mountain of water ahead.

"Damn!" he said, and banked the aircraft to starboard to make another pass. However, when he got back to the position, the U-boat was nowhere to be seen. "Missed him," he said to Flight Sergeant Murphy seated next to him, operating the radar.

"We must have done some damage," replied Murphy. "Those charges were awfully close."

"You're right, make a note in the log: ATTACKED AND DAMAGED U-BOAT POSITION 47-47 NORTH, 49-50 WEST 0930 HOURS."

"Too bad, sir. I really thought we had him," said Murphy.

"So did I, Jim." Collins checked his fuel gauges and compass and returned H-Harry of RCAF Squadron 10 back to her original course, the lumbering aircraft bumping and jerking in the air turbulence as he gained height.

Nine hundred feet below the surface of the North Atlantic, the shattered hull of *U502* came to rest on the seabed. The two depth charges had, in fact, broken her back and ruptured the pressure hull at the engine room. Death came quickly to those in the compartment and aft. However, the pressure tight hatch separating the Engine Room from the Control Room forward held - briefly. At 300 feet, it started to leak and, as the U-boat sank deeper, the terrified occupants of the room watched the flow increase and the hatch start to give way.

Suddenly, it tore from its hinges and a fist of black water punched through the compartment. *Oberfunkmeister* Clausen screamed and raised his arms in a futile gesture as the water hammer reached him. He was thrown against the bulkhead and immediately killed. Shortly, it was over and the earthly remains of fifty men lay entombed in their *Iron Coffin* for eternity.

CHAPTER ELEVEN

LINDA HALLEY SAT ON THE COUCH in the living room, staring vacantly off into space. She wore the same heavy terrycloth bathrobe Mitchell had - she could still smell him on it - and her own blue fuzzy slippers. A cup of tea sat untouched on the table in front of her. Suddenly, Dr. Halley burst into the room looking for his pipe, interrupting Linda's daydream.

"Thinking about your young lieutenant, honey?" he enquired.

"Yes."

"You really like him, don't you?"

"Dad, I love him," said Linda, looking directly at her father.

"That sounds serious, honey. What about Mitch, does he love you?"

"Alistair, Dad. And yes, he does."

"So, what are you going to do about it?" asked the doctor.

"I don't know, Dad. A sailor in wartime isn't what you'd call a safe bet. He could be killed tomorrow, or be transferred to someplace else and I wouldn't see him until the end of the war."

"Honey, there's no such thing as a safe bet," answered her father, going to the mantle. "When your mother and I first met, I was still in med school and didn't have two nickels to rub together. Even after I graduated, we were looking at a couple of years before I could start my own practice, a couple of very lean years."

He found his pipe and started to fill it. "But she took a chance and married me. She could have played it safe and married one of the Clifts or O'Deas, God knows she was asked enough times! Her father even tried to persuade her to wait, at least until I was set up. But no, we were young and in love, and that wasn't your mother's way. She didn't take safe bets; she married me and, to the best of my knowledge, never regretted it." He lit his pipe and threw the match into the fireplace.

"Oh, there were times when things were a little rocky, but we made it through, and you will too, honey. Don't miss an opportunity for happiness by playing it safe. Take a chance. Your mother did," Halley finished.

Linda got up off the couch and hugged her father, her head just reaching his chest. "Oh, Daddy!" she said. "I know why Mom loved you so much, 'cause I do too."

"Good," said Dr. Halley, a little embarrassed by his daughter's display of affection. Not the Catholic way. "Now, go get dressed. It's not proper for a young lady to be lazing about the house in her dressing gown. What if Alistair came back early and saw you like this? He might change his mind," he said, smiling.

"Not a chance," said Linda as she darted out of the room. The Doctor puffed on his pipe and slowly shook his head. Oh boy, he thought, I wish your mother were here now. This is way above my pay grade!

Upstairs, Second Officer Linda Halley WRCNS (*Women in Royal Canadian Naval Service,* better known as Wrens after their British sister group) put on her uniform and checked her appearance in the mirror. Even though she wasn't due to start her shift at Operations until 1100, she was going in anyway to keep her mind off Alistair Mitchell. Privy to all the latest intelligence reports, she was aware of just how dangerous the waters around Newfoundland really were. She knew of the sinkings and U-boat sightings, and even though the ocean escort forces derisively called the local convoys the "Milk Run", they were just as perilous as the much vaunted "North Atlantic Run" or the "Triangle Run" from Halifax to New York, via St. John's. The Port aux Basques to North Sydney ferry had been sunk in early October by a U-boat with a loss of 137 lives, including women and children, the training submarine HMCS *P. 510* had been sunk in error off Cape Race on her way to Harbour Grace, and even HMCS *Valleyfield* had been lost off the South Coast. Linda dabbed her lips with a tissue to remove some excess lipstick and glanced around her bedroom for her handbag. She saw the regulation issue carryall slung on the bedpost and, picking it up, checked for her 'necessities'. God, I'm such a girl, she admonished herself, but with a smile.

Mrs. O'Brien was dusting the entranceway mirror when Linda descended the stairs. Almost sixty, she had slipped into the role of surrogate mother after Mrs. Halley died the year before. Linda was deeply affected by her mother's death and Mrs. O'Brien, being both a woman and a mother, knew that she needed the comfort that her father could not provide, no matter how much he loved her.

"Hi, dearie," she said when she saw Linda.

"Hi, Mrs. O'Brien."

"You're leaving early."

"Yes," said Linda. "I thought I'd go in and catch up on all the latest gossip. I've been off a week so there should be something juicy."

"Maybe a little bit of your own?" said Mrs. O'Brien with a conspiring look.

"Oh, no! That's a secret for the time being." Linda put on her coat, kissed the older lady on the cheek and said, "See you tomorrow."

"Have a good day, dear," said Mrs. O'Brien, as Linda went through the door. God bless your young lieutenant, she thought, he's just what the doctor ordered. She chuckled at her little pun, and went back to her dusting.

Linda walked down the tree-lined driveway and caught the streetcar at the end of the road, where it intersected with Water Street and Waterford Bridge Road. As she sat looking out the window at the grey day, she thought of Mitchell.

She'd been evasive when he had asked her where she worked, afraid if she told him, he might ask her what his new assignment was. She didn't want to lie to him but she wasn't allowed to say anything about what went on in Operations. She knew what his orders were and about the sinkings in September off Bell Island. She also knew Intelligence suspected a spy and that there were several U-boats offshore.

The streetcar arrived at Naval Headquarters on Plymouth Road. The armed sentry checked her identification and held the door for her as he let her through. Off-duty sailors, and even some junior officers, made appreciative noises as she walked in, despite her rank. She showed her identity card to the sentry on duty at the Security Check before proceeding down the hall to the Operations Room. She opened the door and almost collided with Patsy Aylward, her "oppo" at Communications, who was on her way out with an armload of signals.

"Hi, Linda. You look swell! I wonder, would that have anything to do with that lieutenant I saw you with at

Captain (D)'s Cocktail Party Friday night?"

"I never kiss and tell, Patsy, you know that," Linda said with a smile.

"Uh-huh," said Theresa. "Give me a jingle when you get a minute." She bustled out the door and trotted down the hall.

Not a chance, thought Linda. Patsy would have it spread all over the Command in no time. She took off her coat, hung it up on one of the hooks by the door, and looked to her right at the large map which occupied the whole wall. The Plot showed all of the Newfoundland Command's escort forces and aircraft patrols, as well as convoy positions and those of known U-boats.

At the top right was an outbound slow convoy with several escorts plus an air patrol. At the bottom, between the French islands of St. Pierre and Miquelon and the Burin Peninsula, was a small coastal convoy, protected by a minesweeper and two Fairmile patrol boats. Her gaze was drawn to Conception Bay. Five ship silhouettes were in the anchorage between Bell Island and the mainland plus two smaller ones, denoting patrol boats. At the mouth of the Bay was the eighth.

She went to her desk and started reading old signals to catch up on the events of the past week. However, her eyes kept going back to the lone ship's label at the entrance to Conception Bay. All it said was HMCS *Dartmouth*. To Linda, it could have read *Lt. Alistair Mitchell.*

CHAPTER TWELVE

ADMIRAL KARL DÖNITZ read the signal, then balled it up and threw it angrily towards the wastepaper basket in the corner of the Situation Room. He missed, and it fell to the floor. *Kapitän zur See* Eberhard Gödt, Donitz's Chief of Operations, looked up at the Admiral from the tabletop map of the North Atlantic. "Bad news, Admiral?"

"*U502* has been sunk. She was sending a coded weather report when it stopped, then said ATTACKED-AIRCRAFT in plain language, and that was it. That's the third weather-boat sunk over there in as many months!"

"He was off Newfoundland, wasn't he?" stated Gödt, glancing at the map in front of him. On it were the last reported positions of all the U-boats in the North Atlantic.

"Yes," replied Dönitz. "It's getting as bad as the Bay of Biscay for *verdammt* aircraft attacks."

"We have to keep sending boats up there, sir. We need to know what the weather will be to plan convoy operations."

"I know, Eberhard," said Dönitz, irritably, "but we can't afford to lose a boat a month, like we are now. We have to do something about the aircraft out of Newfoundland."

"Sir, any delay would only be temporary," replied the Captain, "and we still need the weather reports on an almost hourly basis. It would solve no...."

"Sir?" interrupted *Kapitän-Leutnant* Günter Hessler, the First Staff Officer. Hessler was an accomplished U-boat skipper with over 100,000 tons of enemy shipping to his credit. He held *Das Ritterkreus* (the Knights Cross of the Iron Cross) and had completed the most successful patrol of the War when the BdU appointed him Staff Officer (Operations). He was also Dönitz's son-in-law.

"Yes, Günter?" enquired the Admiral.

"How about an automated weather station? Land it someplace remote on Newfoundland's coast."

"There are no remote places along Newfoundland's coast. Most of the population live along the coast. They're fishermen, remember?" answered Dönitz.

"Then how about Labrador? No one up there but Eskimos. Well, up north anyway," persisted Hessler.

"That's an idea," said Gödt. *Dönitz's* Chief of Operations was a quiet, thoughtful man, a perfect balance to his boss's more impetuous nature. He often kept in the background during a heated discussion, absorbing all views, before formulating his own opinion. Dönitz trusted him implicitly. "The one we put on Greenland has proven to be very reliable."

"What about the aircraft patrols from Newfoundland? No good if a boat gets sunk on its way there"

"A commando raid?" suggested Hessler.

"What!" exclaimed Dönitz.

Hessler hesitated a moment, gathering his thoughts. He was not intimidated by his father-in-law, far from it. He knew Dönitz to be tough, but good-humoured and very concerned about the well-being of his men. He personally met as many returning U-boats as he could, especially in Lorient, not far from his headquarters. But he also demanded the best from his men, especially his staff officers. He did not suffer fools.

"Well, Admiral," he began, "the Canadian air base is just inland from the coast, between St. John's and a place called Tor Bay." He used a pencil to indicate its location on the map table. "We could land a raiding party, like the British did in Norway - just small arms and explosives. A quick in-and-out operation," Hessler concluded.

"Günter, that would be suicide," said the Admiral. "They'd be slaughtered."

"Not if we arranged a diversion," returned Hessler.

"What kind of diversion, *Kapitän-Leutnant?*" asked Gödt, his bushy eyebrows raised enquiringly. Hessler had their complete attention now.

"If we had a couple of boats on the Grand Banks sending signals at irregular intervals all over the place, that would get someone's attention. We know the Allies can Direction/Find our wireless transmissions the same as we can theirs. The boats could change position right after they sent and it will seem like we're planning a major offensive right off the coast. They'd send every plane and warship they could muster."

"And what would that accomplish, if all the planes were gone? The whole purpose is to destroy them, isn't it?" said Dönitz.

"No, sir," replied Hessler. "The Canadians would just replace any we destroyed with others, maybe from Gander or Argentia. They'd be back in operation within a few days. But, if we seriously damaged the facilities themselves - the hangars and machine shops, the control tower, the fuel dumps, the runways - they'd be paralysed for months or even a year while they rebuilt. It would also distract them from the weather station," Hessler finished.

Dönitz stared at his young protégé, with his piercing blue eyes. Hessler started to feel a little uncomfortable under his superior's unrelenting gaze. But Dönitz wasn't looking at Hessler. He was thinking. Finally, he said, "It might just work, Günter."

Hessler exhaled quietly. He hadn't realized he'd been holding his breath. "Would you like me to prepare an Operation Plan, sir?"

"Yes, Günter, please. As fast as you can. How long will you need?"

"No more than a day, sir."

"Good. See to it."

Hessler said, "Yes, sir," and left.

Dönitz turned to his Chief of Operations. "What do you think, Eberhard? Can it work?"

"Yes, sir," replied Gödt, thoughtfully. "I think it can. It will require a lot of planning and co-ordination but if we can pull it off, it could be a major blow to the Allies in the Western Atlantic."

"I agree," said Dönitz. He stared down at the map table, visualizing the operation in his mind. He looked up at Gödt, "Do we have a boat available that we could convert quickly to a troop carrier?"

"I think so, sir," replied the *Kapitän*. He walked over to a side table and sifted through a stack of flimsies. Finding the one he was looking for, he said, "This boat, sir, *U573*. She's an IXC just in from the Baltic training flotilla."

"Who's her captain?" inquired the Admiral.

"Peter Schilling," answered Gödt.

"He was with Ulrich Fölkers in *U125*, wasn't he? When Fölkers went over, just after the Americans declared war?"

"Yes, sir, I believe he was the First Watch Officer."

Dönitz addressed his Flag Lieutenant, at his elbow. "Rudi, make an appointment for *Kapitän-Leutnant* Schilling to see me tomorrow afternoon." The young man nodded and left to carry out the order. Turning to *Kapitän* Gödt, Dönitz said, changing the topic, "Okay. Now, what's on for tonight?"

CHAPTER THIRTEEN

GENTLY PARTING A SCHOOL OF COD in its path, the U-boat glided silently through the depths. Wassermann sat astride the saddle of the attack periscope in the Conning Tower, his feet operating the pedals controlling its movements. He looked down the hatch connecting the *Turm* to the Control Room below and said, "He's just finished the last leg and is heading back across. Elapsed time, Number One?"

The First Watch Officer, at the bottom of the ladder, glanced at the stopwatch in his hand and, looking up the hatch, called, "Forty-eight minutes, sir!"

Wassermann lowered the periscope and dismounted. He slid down the

ladder to the Control Room and strode
over to the chart table. Tröjer followed
behind him. He picked up a pencil
and, using it as a pointer, said, "That
gives us about fifteen minutes where
he is facing away from this side,"
indicating the western coast of the
Bay. He grabbed the parallel rule and
started some calculations on a clear
space at the bottom of the chart.

U581 reached Conception Bay in
mid-afternoon, having made good
time, even while submerged. The cold
Labrador Current flowing down from
the north added a few extra knots on
to their usual underwater cruising
speed of four knots. Upon arrival,
Wassermann raised the attack
periscope, so-called because its small
diameter made less of a disturbance
on the surface, and immediately
sighted a *destroyer* patrolling the
entrance of the Bay. To German U-
boatmen, anything smaller than a
cruiser but larger than a patrol boat
was termed a destroyer. As far as they
were concerned, whether it was a

destroyer, frigate, or corvette, it still had only one job - to sink U-boats.

Through periodic periscope glimpses, Wassermann ascertained that the warship was sticking to a set patrol pattern which brought him across the mouth of the bay, along the coast for a short distance, and then back across to the other side. Visibility was only fair, a light rain was falling, and the sea was a bit choppy. Not bad conditions for an attack, considering.

Wassermann turned around and faced the crew assembled in the Control Room, his elbows resting on the top of the chart table. He raised the black peak of his white officer's hat, the trademark of a U-boat skipper, and asked for their attention.

"Here's the plan," he started. "We'll go in at midnight, on the surface, hugging the western side when the destroyer is on the eastern leg of his search pattern. We should be invisible against the cliffs and our wake will look like normal surf action. *Oberleutnant* Tröjer and I, plus two lookouts, will be on the bridge. I want

Obergefreiter Klöninger in the tower on helm and *Stabsobersteuermann* Capito with him to convey torpedo firing orders to the Control Room.

"The northern entrance to the anchorage is most likely protected by mines and/or a torpedo net and possibly searchlights and guns. So, we will go around the Island and in through the southern channel between the two small islands. There is probably a patrol boat there but again, against the outline of the shore and the islands, we should be able to dodge it. Once we are inside, we'll pick our targets, sink as many as we can, and escape the same way we came in." Wassermann concluded, "Any questions?"

Mannstein spoke up, "Should we man the *Flakvierling* or the 105mm forward?"

"No," replied Wassermann. "If we're surprised, our best defence is the dark and our high surface speed. Besides, if we have to dive quickly, the least number of men on the bridge, the better." He waited and asked, "Anyone else?" Looking at Tröjer, he asked, "Number One?"

"Sir, I suggest we load one of the new *Zaunkönig* acoustic torpedoes in a stern tube. Just in case we run into the destroyer on the way out."

"Good idea, *Oberleutnant*. See to it, please," answered Wassermann. "Anyone else? No? Good. *Leutnant* Mannstein, you're right. I want *Leutnant* Dietrich and the gunners here in the Control Room too during the action, in case we do have to man the 105 mm forward or the Flakvierling aft. See to it."

"Jawohl, Kaleu," replied the young lieutenant.

"Right, then. We'll surface at nightfall and head out to sea to get a full battery charge and send off a position report. Until then, I want all equipment checked and rechecked. I don't want any dud torpedoes or other foul-ups tonight." Wassermann concluded, "Ready, men?"

In unison the entire Control Room replied, "*Jawohl, Kaleu!*"

Wassermann dodged through the hatch, headed for his cabin. Tröjer went aft to ensure the homing torpedo was loaded. Newly developed, the *Zaunkönig* was designed to follow the noise of an attacking escort's propellers and detonate against them. Electrically powered, it lacked the range, speed, and wallop of the heavier G7a steam-driven torpedo. But it left no tell-tale wake, making it harder to detect and therefore evade. Although it mightn't sink the target, it would certainly stop it, giving the U-boat the chance to escape. The British called it the *Gnat* (for German Naval Acoustic Torpedo) which seemed appropriate. It was the *sting in the tail* a U-boat needed when being hunted.

Leutnant zur See Dietrich smiled somewhat too intensely and tapped out a tattoo with his pencil on the top of the chart table. He could hardly wait!

CHAPTER FOURTEEN

THE WATER WAS PAINFULLY COLD. It sapped the strength from his limbs and seemed to drain his very soul. He struggled to stay afloat as his heavy duffle coat and sea boots tried to drag him down. A wave washed over him, covering his face with fuel oil that stung his eyes and made him gag. He saw other heads in the water with him, many badly burned. In the distance *Dartmouth* was afire and sinking, the night sky brightening as explosions rocked the little warship.

In the glow of the flames, Mitchell saw the cause of his pain and loss. The long, low silhouette of the U-boat cruising among the survivors, machine guns blazing. It turned and came straight for Mitchell, bow wave getting larger as it increased speed. He was

washed along its cold iron sides, water filling his lungs, the suction of the fast-moving propellers dragging him under. He heard his name, and there, on the deck of the U-boat, screaming and kicking as she was being dragged along by two Nazi sailors, was Linda Halley, her hair thick with oil and her eyes wild. He desperately clawed at the casing of the submarine but was swept closer and closer to the churning water at the stern. He called her name as the propellers pulled him down and the dark water closed over his head.

Mitchell sat bolt upright in his bunk. His heart was racing and his body trembled. Sweat dampened his clothes. It was nightime, and he stared wide-eyed into the darkness, trying to get his bearings. A nightmare! Just a nightmare, he realized. Like all the others over the past two years, just different players.

He swung out of the bunk and looked out the scuttle. It was overcast and a light rain was falling. *Dartmouth* swayed slightly under his feet as she rode the swells. With shaking hands he pulled the blackout curtain across the port, and turned on the overhead light. He took a cigarette from the pack on his desk, lit it with shaking hands, and sat back down on the side of the bunk, the images of the dream still fresh in his mind. Mitchell looked at his watch. 1800. I've slept all day, he thought.

He heard activity next door in the officers' pantry and, assuming it was McDonald, Mitchell picked up the telephone and called. The steward answered and Mitchell asked him for a sandwich and a mug of tea to take to the bridge. McDonald said, "Right away,

sir," and Mitchell hung up. He changed out of his damp shirt and was just putting on his duffle coat when McDonald came in with his supper.

"You all right, sir?" he asked, noticing Mitchell's pasty face.

"Yes, fine, thank you, McDonald. These all-night watches wear me out," lied Mitchell. "Who has the bridge?"

"Lieutenant Blandford, sir. Lieutenant Porter's in the wardroom having supper and Lieutenant Martin is asleep." He paused. "Can I get you anything else, sir?"

"No, I'm fine, thanks. Give Lieutenant Blandford my compliments and tell him I'll join him shortly."

"Yes, sir," replied McDonald and left.

Mitchell went over to the basin on the wall, turned on the tap and splashed cold water on his face. He was awake now and the effects of the nightmare were diminishing. He brushed his teeth and combed his hair. Staring at his reflection in the mirror, he thought, a bit better, surprised at how much the nightmare had shaken him.

ON THE BRIDGE, Lieutenant Blandford, known as "Guns", as were most gunnery officers, nodded at

McDonald's message. He preferred to have the bridge to himself but, with the coming of night, he had expected the Captain's presence. Not that he disliked Mitchell. Overall, he was a good captain and generally let his officers do their jobs with the minimum of interference, but he wasn't very adventurous. Also like most gunnery officers, Blandford would rather charge into a situation, guns blazing for guts and glory, whereas Mitchell was more thoughtful and cautious. Maybe that was why in thirteen months of constant duty, *Dartmouth* had yet to even assist in the sinking of a U-boat. Lieutenant Blandford didn't consider the "safe and timely arrival of the convoy" as a measure of success, only U-boat silhouettes on the forward bridgescreen, marking the number of subs sunk. And there isn't much chance of anything happening here, he thought ruefully. Mitchell arrived on the bridge. "Evening, Guns. All quiet?"

"As a churchyard, sir."

"Good," replied Mitchell, getting into his chair and resting his mug of tea on the arm.

"Sir, don't you find this all very boring?"

"Guns, I'd rather die of boredom in my living room at seventy than right now of a torpedo up the arse. Wouldn't you?" Mitchell grimaced, the nightmare suddenly remembered.

"I guess so, sir," he answered dubiously. "But I'd at least like to see a U-boat."

"Don't worry. This is going to be a long war. You'll get your chance, yet." Mitchell changed the topic. "What's the word from the anchorage?"

"*PBM27, Fort Rose,* and *Mary P* anchored offshore, and *Spring Valley* and *Pilos* loading. *Q075* is patrolling the southern channel and *Q087* is in reserve. All is quiet as of 1800," Blandford finished.

"Let's hope it stays that way, Guns," said Mitchell. You can count on it, thought Blandford, but said instead, "Yes, sir."

CHAPTER FIFTEEN

THE BOAT WAS QUIET, the reassuring throb of the diesels felt rather than heard as one engine propelled the boat at eight knots. The other poured vital electricity into the huge, two ton lead batteries under the deck plates of the forward accommodation spaces. Most of the crew were in their bunks, re-reading old letters or writing new ones. Some looked at dog-eared photographs of loved ones - wives, children, girlfriends. No one slept.

In the Wardroom, just forward of the Captain's curtained-off cubby-hole, the only sounds were the occasional click of the compass repeater on the bulkhead or gurgle of water being pumped out of the bilges. Periodically, someone in an adjacent compartment coughed, as the oily, fetid air caught in his throat.

Tröjer slid into the bench seat, a mug of *ersatz* coffee in his hand. He hated the stuff, but it was all they had. He nodded to *Leutnant* Mannstein across the table from him, reached into the tin in the centre and took a cigarette. He lit it and inhaled deeply. Exhaling, he took a sip of coffee and pulled a face.

"*Gott*, I hate this stuff," he said.

"I hear that the boats out of France have the real thing," Mannstein replied. "Funny, isn't it? In Germany we have to drink this crap, and the Frenchies have the genuine article. Who's the victor and who's the vanquished? And don't give me that *the Vichy French are our allies* BS. I know better."

Tröjer looked at him. "Do you ever wonder if we'll win, Wolf? This was supposed to be a quick, painless war, remember? We all clambered to get to sea before it was over. To get our share of sinkings! Everyone was going to get a Knight's Cross." Tröjer paused. "Now, three years later, we're still at it and no closer to victory."

"I don't know, Gerd," said Mannstein, looking into his cup. "I hope so or Germany will be destroyed. They'll carve us up like a piece of steak. How would you like to be part of the Soviet Union, Comrade Tröjerski?" Mannstein lifted his eyebrows inquiringly.

"Not funny, Wolfgang."

"Sorry, I forgot about Ingrid and the baby. With her parents, are they?"

"Yes," replied Tröjer, rubbing his face with his hands.

"Have they been bombed yet?"

"Hannover has, but Krefeld is too small for the British to bother with."

"My family is in Dresden. I guess they're safe enough, nothing there of any military importance. How about you? Think we'll win?" asked Mannstein.

"I'm beginning to doubt it, Wolf. We're alone against the whole world. Our allies...well, Mussolini was fine when he was slaughtering half-naked tribesmen in Ethiopia but, if it weren't for Rommel, we would have lost North Africa long ago. And the Japs, they've got their hands full with the Americans."

"Two years ago, we were annihilating whole convoys with just a few boats - remember Günter Prien, Silent Otto...Schepke? Now we're sneaking into a defended harbour to get at three or four lousy ore carriers." Tröjer looked at his folded hands, "I'm afraid we're losing!"

"That's enough, *Oberleutnant!*" Both men looked up. Wassermann stood in the doorway. "I'll thank you to keep your defeatist views to yourself."

"Sir," said Tröjer, "they're not defeatist. They are the views of a patriot who is also a worried husband and father."

"Number One, if we have trust in our leaders and do our duty, we have nothing to fear," lectured Wassermann.

"Do you really believe that, sir?" asked Mannstein, raising an eyebrow towards Tröjer.

"I have to, *Leutnant*," said Wassermann, softening. "Otherwise, how would I keep going? You're worried about your wife and son," he said, looking at his Second-in-Command, but including Mannstein. "I have the lives of fifty men to worry about. How about their wives and sons, and daughters, and parents? Gentlemen, we are fighting for our lives now. You are right, *Oberleutnant* Tröjer. We are alone against the world, and God help us if we lose."

Wassermann paused, reached over to the can of cigarettes on the table, and took one. He lit it and, through a cloud of smoke, continued, "Our only chance for survival now is to make it too costly for the Allies to defeat us. That is why we're going into Conception Bay tonight, *Oberleutnant.* Why we're going to sink as many ships as we can. If we can make fighting us too expensive, then maybe the British and Americans, and Canadians, will sue for peace. Even if we lose everything we've gained in three years of war, at least Germany won't be destroyed. Think of it that way." He looked again at Tröjer, "When we go in there tonight, Number One, you are fighting for your wife and son, as surely as if you were standing in front of their door with a loaded *Schmeisser*."

"Yes, sir," said Tröjer, somewhat sheepishly.

"Now," said Wassermann, "having made my little speech, let's make sure nothing goes wrong tonight. I don't want to end up on the bottom of Conception Bay!"

Both men replied, "Yes, sir," and extinguished their cigarettes. Tröjer slid out, off the bench, followed by Mannstein. Wassermann stood aside as they went through the doorway.

He sat down, and noticed his hands were trembling. He took a cigarette from the can and lit it off the smouldering end of the one in his fingers. He crushed out the butt and sat smoking quietly, waiting for the shakes to stop. After a few minutes they did. He put out his smoke, got up, and headed for the Control Room.

PAQUETTE CONCLUDED HIS SIGNOFF MESSAGE and received an acknowledgement, then shut down the transmitter and pushed back his chair. He lit a cigarette and looked at his watch. Five after eleven. He got up and turned off the overhead light as he went through the door on his way to the bridge.

All was quiet when he got there. The only light, the soft glow from the engine telegraphs and the compass. They'd finished loading close to midnight, the night before, and had moved out into the anchorage before first light. Captain Garros was still ashore but most of the crew were now on board.

Second Officer Jean Carrier had the bridge. Carrier was just a young man, not much older than Paquette, and more approachable than Bligh. He was usually in a good mood and was not above laughing at a joke, no matter how off-coloured. He smiled when he saw Paquette come up the stairs to the bridge.

"Good evening, François," he said. "Calling it a night?"

"Thought I'd have a coffee and a smoke first. Would you like one?"

"Sure. Why not? No sugar."

Paquette headed below to the galley. It was deserted except for Ban Ban, who was behind the counter making bread. He nodded to Paquette and continued kneading the dough while humming some out of tune song to himself. Paquette went over to the rack, took a couple of mugs and filled them at the coffee urn. He put sugar and tinned milk in his and just milk in the other, then stirred both. He bid good night to the baker, who again just nodded, still humming, and headed forward to the bridge. When he got there, he passed Carrier his mug with his fingertips, and took out a pack of cigarettes. After offering it to Carrier, who took one, he took a smoke for himself and lit both with his lighter. Carrier mumbled his thanks and looked out the bridge windows at the dark bulk of Bell Island.

"We'll be in Sydney by tomorrow night, François. I suppose you'll be sampling the wine and the women," he said.

"In Sydney?" retorted Paquette, raising an eyebrow. "You?"

"Oh, no. I'm married."

Paquette looked at him, brow furrowed. "I didn't know that. Where is she, in England?"

"Lorient. With my little girl, Monique. I haven't heard from them since the war started," said Carrier quietly. "I hope they're all right."

"I'm sure they are," said Paquette. "Why wouldn't they be?"

"My wife is Jewish," said Carrier. "I've heard the Boche are rounding up all the Jews, loading them into cattle cars, then sending them to concentration camps in Poland. The bastards! My wife isn't well and Monique is only five." He looked at Paquette. "I would die if anything happened to them, François!"

Paquette looked down at his mug. "I'm sorry, Jean. I didn't know."

"Don't be, François. My wife doesn't look Jewish and hasn't been in a synagogue in years. I'm probably worrying about nothing." Carrier sipped his coffee.

"I hope so, Jean," Paquette said, disturbed. "I really do. Well, I'd better get below. I'm back on duty at six-thirty." He snuffed out his cigarette.

"Sure," said Carrier. "See you in the morning."

Paquette went below, dropping into the mess to leave his dirty mug. Chan was still there. He continued aft until he came to the cabin he shared with two other men, both on duty in the engine room. He lay on his bunk and thought of his conversation with Carrier.

Paquette had also heard about the Jews and the concentration camps; the massacres and other atrocities in France, Belgium, and the Netherlands. He was Vichy-French, yes, but the *Wehrmacht* seemed to be more of a conquering force now, rather than the liberator of oppressed peoples, as Paquette has previously thought when he'd first started working for the Germans. War was one thing, thought Paquette, soldiers against soldiers, machines against machines, but using civilians as hostages, and shipping innocent men, women, and children off for slave labour was something else. It was an hour before he finally fell asleep.

LEADING SEAMAN TOM GARRETT sat with his feet up on the desk, reading a paperback, cigarette burning unnoticed in the ashtray. Things were usually quiet in the Communications Room this time of night and Tom, an avid reader, spent most of his shift with his nose buried in a book. Without warning, the teletype machine in the corner started to churn out a message, interrupting Garrett's reading.

He swung his legs off the desk. He picked up his cigarette, took one last drag, and put it out. He got up, stretched, and headed over to the machine. Lifting the top of the sheet as the message completed, he read:

U-BOAT TRANSMISSION D/F 48-50N, 52-50W 2200HRS TODAY

BELIEVED SAME U-BOAT D/F 31OCT OFF LAB

H.F./D.F. STATION MAIN SENDS

Garrett tore off the sheet and headed down the hall to the office of Lieutenant Frank Ryan, RCNVR, Night Duty Officer for the Office of Naval Intelligence (Newfoundland Command). He knocked on Ryan's door and, without waiting for an answer, entered. Ryan looked up and said, not unpleasantly, "What is it, Killick?" He and Garrett had known each other for a while.

Passing Ryan the signal, Garrett replied, "The Huff Duff boys have pinpointed another U-boat, sir."

"Yeah?" said Ryan.

Frank Ryan had been a reporter before the war, and a damn good one. He had a logical mind and could piece together seemingly unrelated clues to get to the bottom of any story. This talent was further enhanced by a stubborn streak; he never let anything slide. He continued to ponder a problem long after his superiors had deemed it superfluous. His friends at the newspaper called him Sherlock.

Ryan read the telex and said, "So, our friend up north is on the move. Heading home or just changing areas?"

He dismissed Garrett, got up, and went to the map of Newfoundland on the wall. There were a half a dozen red-balled push pins stuck into the map, denoting the positions of U-boats known to be in the area covered by the Newfoundland Command. Two were off the west coast, in the Gulf of St. Lawrence; two were further south; one was out by the Flemish Cap, three hundred miles east of St. John's; and the other one, the one Ryan was concerned with, off the coast of Labrador.

These fixes came from a variety of sources, including sightings by patrolling aircraft, attacks on convoys, and High Frequency Direction Finding - Huff Duff for short.

The Canadians and Americans had set up a number of radar and Huff Duff stations along the coasts of Newfoundland and Labrador to pinpoint the locations of U-boats by triangulating their radio transmissions between known co-ordinates. It was fairly accurate and gave the Command a chance to reroute convoys or dispatch a warship or aircraft to attack the unsuspecting sub.

Ryan took the pin from the coast of Labrador and placed it at the position indicated in the signal. Well now, he thought, that puts him about twenty miles northeast of Conception Bay. We'll have to keep an eye on you.

He entered the message, then date, in the log on his desk: 2 November, 1942.

CHAPTER SIXTEEN

WASSERMANN WAS ONCE AGAIN ASTRIDE the saddle of the attack periscope. Through the eyepiece he could see HMCS *Dartmouth*, silhouetted against the night sky, commence the return leg of her search pattern. It was still raining lightly but visibility had improved. They'd dived an hour before, for the transit into the coast, and were now at fifteen metres awaiting the moment to penetrate the bay.

Wassermann was alone in the Conning Tower but the Control Room was filled to capacity. In addition to the crewmen manning their stations, there were the two lookouts, Chief Petty Officer Capito, and Action Helmsman Klöninger. All the officers were also present, including *Leutnant* Roenneberg who was supervising the planesmen and controlling the trim.

"He's starting the eastern leg of his patrol," stated Wassermann. He lowered the periscope, jumped off the saddle and slid down the ladder to the Control Room. "Prepare to surface," he ordered.

Tröjer climbed the ladder to the tower followed closely by the two lookouts, all clad in oilskins.

"Surface!"

Immediately, a well-rehearsed ballet of controlled confusion commenced. The diving planes were put Hard Arise and compressed air thundered into the main ballast tanks, starting with the one in the bow. Valves were opened, then shut in series, wheels spun and switches turned on or off.

Roenneberg started counting off the depth in metres before finally saying, "Hatch is clear."

Wassermann yelled over the racket, "Crack the hatch, secure compressed air, start engines!"

As quickly as it had started, the mad blasting of air ceased and the last of the lookouts disappeared up the ladder. Back aft in the engine room, *Dieselmaat* Hirschfeld spun the wheels opening the large engine induction vents located under the *Wintergarten* at the rear of the Conning Tower above. As *Diesel-Obermaschinist* Frauenheim pushed the starters, in the next compartment *Electro-Obermaschinist* Keller shut down the electric motors.

The rumble of the massive engines could be heard forward in the Control Room, despite the closed hatch between, and the deck vibrated purposefully beneath their feet. Wassermann ordered, "Ahead standard, both. Commence low pressure blow." The ballast tanks were never fully emptied by the compressed air and the exhaust from the engines was used to complete the job. The Captain wanted the U-boat at full surface trim in case they had to make a quick exit. The less hull underwater, the less drag, hence more speed.

Wassermann put on his rubber rain gear and climbed the ladder to the bridge. He arrived just as the two lookouts were reporting "all clear" to *Oberleutnant* Tröjer.

"All clear, *Kaleu*!" repeated Tröjer. Tröjer had never addressed Wassermann as that before.

"Very good, Number One," said Wassermann, noticing the change in salutation.

In the distance to port, the bridge crew could see *Dartmouth*'s stern with its wake of disturbed water trailing behind. Wassermann opened the voicepipe and ordered *Obergefreiter* Klöninger below in the Conning Tower to "Steer 230." Tröjer took his station astern on the *Wintergarten* while forward, Wassermann raised his binoculars in a vain attempt to see Bell Island. *U581* was on her way to Wabana.

"STEADY ON 110, SIR," reported Sub-Lieutenant Martin, who had relieved Lieutenant Blandford shortly before.

"Very good," acknowledged Mitchell.

Unlike Blandford, Martin was happy to have Mitchell on the bridge with him. Barely nineteen and, despite six months' active duty on *Dartmouth*, Martin still lacked confidence in his ability to handle a life and death emergency if it arose. He felt quite capable in handling the ship and the men, and did not follow the tradition of most sub-lieutenants in equating authority with the volume of one's voice. Consequently, most of the crew liked the young man and few gave him any trouble. Despite that, he appreciated the safety net of having the Skipper to turn to if anything happened.

Mitchell sat in his high wooden Captain's chair surveying the coast with his binoculars. He couldn't see much, just the dark outline of the cliffs and the white water of the surf below. All looked normal. But then it would. An intruder would be as unobtrusive as possible, and Mitchell was just looking for some small indication that a U-boat might be in his path. A swirl of a periscope being lowered or a wave going in a different direction than its neighbours, was all he needed. But no, all seemed in order.

He still had an uneasy feeling, a premonition. Maybe it was the lingering effects of this afternoon's nightmare, he thought. However, he picked up the telephone and dialled the Radar/Asdic Room directly below his feet.

"Vaughan," was the reply.

"Captain, Chief," said Mitchell. "Anything on sound or radar?"

"Nothing, sir," came the report. "The cliffs are all that's showing up on radar and the odd ghost, probably a wavetop. And we're getting a lot of bottom return on Asdic. It's a bit too shallow here, sir, especially as we approach shore."

"Okay, keep me posted, Chief."

"Will do, sir!" answered Chief Petty Officer Vaughan.

Dartmouth reached the point just off the coast where she would turn south and follow the shoreline for about ten minutes. Mitchell leaned back in his chair and heard Martin give instructions to the man at the wheel. The ship heeled slightly to starboard as she changed course, but straightened shortly thereafter.

Mitchell gathered his damp coat around him and attempted to get more comfortable. The rain had stopped but nevertheless it was slightly overcast and still damned cold. It was going to be another long night, he thought.

PBM27 STRAINED AT HER ANCHOR CHAIN as she drifted gently with the tide. Down below in his cabin, François Paquette was having his own nightmare.

Men in black uniforms with silver Death's Head emblems on their caps were herding women and children into cattle cars under the glare of floodlights. The children were crying and the women held them close as if to protect them from the blond young men with the machine guns. A little boy slipped and fell, scraping his knee on the rough concrete surface of the train platform. One of the soldiers lifted him gently to his feet and gave him to his mother who looked inquiringly into the young man's eyes. He couldn't meet her gaze and turned back to join his comrades. An officer, with black riding crop slapping against his immaculate black boots, strode up the platform yelling orders. The soldiers, including the one who had helped the little boy, started pushing the miserable assemblage roughly into the cattle cars, sliding the doors shut with a final thump, sealing their fates.

Paquette felt a hand on his shoulder and was instantly awake, his skin feverish and wet with sweat.

"Wake up, *mon ami*! You are having a nightmare." It was LaPoile, one of his roommates.

"Are...are you off duty?" stammered Paquette. "Is it time for me to get up?"

"*Mon Dieu*, no my friend, it's only 0200," LaPoile chuckled.

"Why are you back then? Is something wrong?" asked Paquette, alarmed, remembering September's sinkings and last night's message.

"No, nothing's wrong. I just forgot my smokes and came back for them first chance I got. Relax, François. Go back to sleep. But have better dreams, eh. Think of the women we'll see in Sydney tomorrow." LaPoile turned and left.

Paquette muttered, "Good night," but did not go back to sleep. He lay in his bunk, staring at the underside of the one above him.

On the bridge, Jean Carrier lit a cigarette and thought of his wife and little girl. He walked out onto the bridge wing and stared at the dark water below. After this trip, he thought, I've got to get back to France and find them. I wonder would the British parachute me in if I promised to keep in touch? He would talk to Garros in the morning. His mind made up, he went back to the bridge and looked at the chronometer on the wall. 0205.

CHAPTER SEVENTEEN

U581 HAD PENETRATED DEEP INTO CONCEPTION BAY. She was just rounding the southern tip of Bell Island in preparation for entering the anchorage through the narrow passage between Kelly's Island and Little Bell Island. Despite being on the surface for almost two hours, they had not been detected. Periodically, headlights ran along the highway on the cliffs above, but no alarm was raised. Wassermann quietly gave steering orders to Klöninger below, adjusting their course slightly to have the shadow of one of the islands between them and the anchorage.

They slowed to three knots and entered the "Tickle", as the stretch of water between Bell Island and

Portugal Cove was locally known. Ahead, at the northern passage, spotlights beams were defused by the thin mist. One headed for *U581* and Wassermann altered course to starboard, worried that they'd finally been discovered. It veered away and the U-boat resumed its original path. Behind the wash of the floodlights, the shadows of several ships were seen - one directly ahead at about 500 metres, another 800 metres behind that, and the third approximately 800 metres to port.

Tröjer was now forward at the UZO, the *Unterseeboot Zieloptik*, or U-boat target sights, used on the surface and connected directly to the torpedo director in the Control Room. Wassermann, standing next to him, leaned over and whispered, "Aim for the furthest one first, then we'll swing to port and line up on the other two."

"Jawohl, *Kaleu*," answered Tröjer, and targeted the sights on the ship directly ahead. He leaned over the open hatch at his feet and saw Capito's waiting face. The only light, both on the bridge and in the Conning Tower, was that given off by the gyrocompass and the engine revolutions repeater. "Tube 1, prepare to fire," he whispered unnecessarily, and heard the Petty Officer repeat it to the *Zentrale* below.

As the sights came on, Tröjer ordered, "Los!"

There was a small disturbance forward at the bow of the U-boat and she stalled, ever so briefly. Below, in the bow torpedo room, the compressed air used to fire the tube was vented back into the submarine to prevent a large bubble from erupting on the surface. Not a major consideration in the current circumstance, but deadly if the boat were submerged and it revealed their presence to a patrolling warship. The torpedomen heard a sound under the deck plates, similar to a toilet flushing, and knew it was the torpedo compensating tank adjusting, with seawater, the loss of two tons of torpedo. This prevented the bow from rising uncontrollably, also revealing their position, or deflecting the eel from its intended course.

Immediately, Wassermann gave the orders down the voicepipe to start the evolution to port. The bow started to swing towards the next steamer, at which point Tröjer ordered, "Tubes 2 and 3, prepare to fire." He paused. "Fire!" Two rapid expulsions followed and Tröjer whirled around to line up on the next ship. "Tube 4, prepare to fire." The bow pointed directly at the last target and Tröjer shouted, "Fire!"

Wassermann yelled down the voicepipe, "Full speed, steer 220," heading *U581* between Little Bell Island and its larger namesake.

Tröjer ran to the *Wintergarten* and put his binoculars to his eyes. He plainly saw the track of the first torpedo on the surface as it just missed the bow of the first ship and exploded ashore with a tremendous bang. Starshells and flares immediately illuminated the anchorage, turning the night to day. Twin detonations heralded the destruction of the next target, which shortly rolled over and sank.

Tröjer trained his binoculars to port just in time to see the fourth torpedo find its mark. It hit amidships and, in the light of the explosion, Tröjer saw the letters *PBM27* on the side of the ship. He said, "*Mein Gott!*" and looked at Wassermann.

"What is it, Number One?" asked Wassermann, alarmed.

"That last ship was the *PBM*27, the one we were supposed to avoid," answered Tröjer.

"Tough luck, *Oberleutnant*. There's nothing we can do about it. Our priority now is to get the hell out of here!"

"Yes, sir!" replied Tröjer.

U581 hugged the southern end of Bell Island and headed north out into the bay, keeping to the centre channel. The chart showed it as having a depth of upwards of 250 metres, just in case.

THE TORPEDO HIT *PBM27* dead centre, breaking her back and quickly filling the holds with water. The explosion travelled upwards through the galley, killing Ban-Ban, who had just taken his freshly baked bread out of the oven. It exhausted its destructive force through the top deck, just abaft the bridge, demolishing the radio shack along the way.

Jean Carrier, the lone occupant of the bridge, rushed to the starboard bridge wing at the detonation of the first torpedo ashore. He gaped in horror as the *Fort Rose*, just ahead, exploded in front of him with a large flash. When his eyes again adjusted to the gloom, he watched her roll over and start to sink. He heard a buzzing noise and, looking down, saw a torpedo track intersect with the side of the *PBM27*. He didn't hear the explosion but felt himself thrown over the bridge wing into the water, thirty feet below.

By the time he'd clawed his way back to the surface, the vessel was already on her way to the bottom. To avoid being sucked down with her, Carrier swam away as fast as he could, feeling the internal explosions of the dying ship in his bowels. As he reached the end of his endurance in the frigid water, he banged into a hatch cover, thrown clear by the force of the torpedo's detonation. With the last of his reserves, he pulled himself up onto it and collapsed. Being so close to Bell Island, he knew he'd be rescued, if he could just hang on until morning. He thought of his Monique, but still shivered with the cold.

Paquette was sitting on the side of his bunk smoking a cigarette when the torpedo struck. It threw him violently to the deck where he watched, terrified, as it bulged upwards beneath him. The bulkhead in front of him started to buckle and the light went out. He reached for the door but it was stuck solid, jammed between the distorted frame. He felt water on the floor and, turning, heard the blacked-out glass of the scuttle behind him start to fracture under the fierce outside pressure. It finally imploded, filling the cabin with ice-cold water. Paquette struggled briefly but soon his lifeless body floated upwards to the overhead.

The *PBM27* settled gently into the soft bottom, 100 feet below the surface of Conception Bay.

THE MEN ON THE OPEN BRIDGE of HMCS Dartmouth saw the flashes shortly before the sound of the explosions reached them. They stared open-mouthed as the entire horizon south lit up.

"Oh, my God!" somebody swore.

Mitchell vaulted out of his chair to the starboard side of the bridge and yelled, "Action Stations!"

He turned when he felt the presence of Lieutenant Porter beside him. Porter, like his captain, always slept fully clothed, needing only to slip into his sea boots and put on his duffle coat before reaching the bridge.

"He got by us," was all Porter said.

"Yes, he did," replied Mitchell, without looking at him.

"Shall we head for the anchorage?"

"No," replied Mitchell. "There's nothing we can do there now."

Peters burst onto the bridge. "Sir, R/T from *Q087*. Two ships torpedoed, pier   demolished.   Awaiting instructions."

Mitchell thought for a second, then said, "Tell them to stay where they are and pick up survivors."

To Porter he said, "In this temperature, anyone in the water will only last an hour or so at most, even with a lifebelt."

Back to Peters, "Tell them we'll cover the entrance and try to get the sub on its way out." Peters nodded and left.

Mitchell looked at Porter again and said, "John, you take the bridge." Glancing around he asked, "Where's Lieutenant Martin?"

"Right here, sir!" said Martin, behind him.

"Sub, go below and take charge of the radar and Asdic. He could be on the surface or submerged, so report anything, understand?"

"Yes, sir. Anything," Martin repeated and ran off the bridge.

Blandford strode up to Mitchell. "Oh, Guns," said Mitchell. "Good. You stay here and coordinate the depth charge crew. I also want the 4-incher manned."

"Already done, sir!" said Blandford with a satisfied smile. He walked over to the side of the bridge, put on a headset with microphone attached, and quietly started giving directions into it.

Mitchell walked over to the small chart table, Porter in tow. He leaned over slightly to see better in the dim light and put his forefinger on the centre of the chart.

Looking at his First Lieutenant, he said, "He'll probably head out through here. If he's surfaced, it's the fastest route and if he's submerged, it's the deepest part of the Bay."

"Wouldn't he come out the same way he went in?" asked Porter.

"No. He most likely came in close to shore on the surface, taking advantage of the cliffs, probably when we were heading the other way. But that took time and there's not much depth there if he has to dive. No, he'll come out through the middle, like *a bat out of hell*." Mitchell looked up at Porter, "And we'll be waiting for him."

Mitchell turned to the cox'n at the wheel, "Brodrick, steer 180. Maximum revolutions."

"Steer 180. Maximum revolutions. Aye, sir," repeated Brodrick, turning the wheel and shifting the engine room telegraph.

"Very good," acknowledged Mitchell.

He turned to Blandford, "Guns, make sure they load armour-piercing shells up forward. We won't get too many shots off before he dives, but if we can put a hole in the pressure hull, he's ours."

"Got it, sir," said Blandford.

"Good," said Mitchell. "Let's hope you get to see your U-boat, Guns."

Druken, the bridge telephone talker suddenly spoke up. "Sir, Lieutenant Martin reports a fast-moving target dead ahead, 2000 yards and closing."

Mitchell said to Blandford, "Wait until you have visual contact before you open fire, Guns. It may be one of the Fairmiles."

"Yes, sir," said Blandford and spoke into the microphone.

Mitchell climbed back up into his chair and stared intently forward, trying to see the target through the dark.

Druken counted down the range, "1800....1700...." The moon is out so we should start to see him at 1000 yards, thought Mitchell.

"....1200....1000."

Out of the dark came the white water of a bow wave. Mitchell stood up, trying to determine if the target was, in fact, the U-boat. The bow above the wave became more distinct; pointed, its sharp leading edge slicing through the water. The long, low deck beyond and, about halfway down, the Conning Tower, standing up like the fin of a shark.

Mitchell said, "Now, Guns."

Blandford gave the order and the 4" gun forward barked. But at a combined speed of over thirty knots, the two warships were closing rapidly and, in the dark, it was difficult to properly judge the range. The shot went over and Blandford relayed corrections to the gun crew below. The gun fired again but Mitchell could see plumes of spray along the sides of the U-boat and her bow start to go under. She was diving. "Guns," he said, "prepare for depth charge attack. Set depth at a hundred feet! Maybe we can blow him back to the surface."

CHAPTER EIGHTEEN

HEADING STRAIGHT DOWN the centre of Conception Bay, *U581* was at her top speed of eighteen knots. Wassermann was counting on the patrolling warship going directly to the anchorage via the shortest route - namely the northern entrance, now alight with flares and spotlights. It should miss them in the dark, he thought.

Suddenly, Tröjer yelled, "Destroyer, dead ahead!"

"Alarm!" shouted Wassermann, down the voicepipe.

The two lookouts dived down the hatch, followed by Tröjer. The vents along the sides of the U-boat opened, allowing the air to escape out of the ballast tanks. Below, *Leutnant*

Roenneburg yelled, "All hands forward!" in an attempt to speed up the dive. The quickest way to do this was to increase the weight forward and the most mobile ballast available was the crew itself. Every free man raced forward, diving through hatchways and slipping on the steel deck in a frenzied attempt to get the boat under, and hopefully, out of danger.

Dartmouth's 4" gun opened fire and Wassermann heard the shell whistle overhead and detonate in the wake astern He jumped down the hatch, halting his descent only long enough to dog it closed before continuing down to the Control Room.

At a diving speed of eighteen knots, the U-boat was underwater in thirty seconds and when Wassermann reached the Control Room, they were already at twenty metres. Men were starting to return to their stations to bring the U-boat back on an even keel.

"Sixty metres, Chief," he said to Roenneberg. "Fast!"

Roenneberg gave quiet directions to the two planesmen in front of him and they all heard the fast *thum, thum, thum* of *Dartmouth*'s single screw as she roared overhead.

Klein forward, now on the hydrophones, his head encased in thick rubber earphones, screamed, "Depth charges dropped!"

All hands braced themselves for the horror to follow. Wassermann stared at the depth gauge, as if willing the U-boat deeper.

The first charge detonated forward, as they passed 40 metres, with the remainder following in quick succession. The U-boat rocked violently, men were thrown to the deck and light bulbs burst. Over the noise, Wassermann heard *Leutnant* Roenneberg report, "Sixty metres, sir."

Wassermann ordered, "Dead slow, Chief. Silence throughout the boat! Helmsman, steer 295! Let's see if we can lose her."

ABOVE, *DARTMOUTH* TURNED and resumed her original track. All hands not occupied on the bridge stared into the seething water ahead, looking for signs of success: oil, wreckage, bodies. Nobody saw anything except dead fish, and Mitchell ordered Slow Ahead and a complete Asdic sweep. Martin soon reported a slow-moving contact to port and *Dartmouth* sped up to deliver another attack.

Mitchell said to Blandford, "Guns, set charges to 150 feet."

BELOW, THE CREW OF *U581* could hear *Dartmouth* increase speed in preparation for another drop. As she came closer, Wassermann quietly ordered, "Starboard ten degrees, seventy metres."

Klein yelled, "Charges dropped!" and the crew prepared for another onslaught.

The next barrage was accurately placed but well above the U-boat. The noise was terrific, however the boat shook only slightly. Wassermann looked at Tröjer and smiled, "They know where we are but not how deep."

"Should we fire the *Zaunkönig*, sir?" asked Tröjer.

"Not yet. That's the trick up our sleeve, Number One. Let's wait and see what happens."

ON *DARTMOUTH*'S BRIDGE all hands stared at the frothing water astern. "Sir, target has changed course," reported Druken. "Now heading 305."

"Steer 140. Let's give her another pattern," ordered Mitchell.

"Guns, set depth at 200 feet. Full speed, Lieutenant Porter!"

WASSERMANN HEARD THE CORVETTE charge in. "*Oberleutnant* Tröjer," he said, "maybe it is time for your torpedo."

"Yes, sir," replied Tröjer.

"On my order, please, Number One," said Wassermann calmly.

Dartmouth roared overhead and Klein once again yelled, "Charges dropped!"

This time, the attack was devastating.

The U-boat staggered. Lights went out and men were thrown against the myriad of pipes and wheels. In the motor room, fuses blew and an electrical fire filled the air with choking smoke. The motors stopped turning the propellers. Just forward, in the engine room, the air intake trunking collapsed and the compartment started to fill with water. Reports of damage and flooding came streaming into the Control Room from all over the boat.

Wassermann could smell the unmistakable odour of chlorine. Seawater must have leaked into the forward battery compartment, mixing with the sulphuric acid to produce the deadly gas. U581 was sinking and, if they didn't drown, they would certainly be asphyxiated. That is, if the hull didn't collapse first!

Maximum operating depth was only 150 metres.

"Now, Number One!" ordered Wassermann.

Tröjer pressed the firing button and a slight increase in air pressure preceded the report from the aft room that the torpedo was on its way. "Let's hope it works," was all he said.

Roenneberg started to recite the depth, "120 metres....130 metres....140 metres."

The U-boat creaked and groaned under the intense pressure as she sank deeper and the hull compressed. The deck plates heaved upwards under their feet, warping the ladder to the Conning Tower. A rivet shot across the Control Room with a loud report, smashing the glass face of the depth gauge in front of the planesmen. A sudden crump sounded overhead. One of the pressure-tight containers in the casing had imploded. Men glanced furtively at each other in the faint light, loath to show their fear lest it cause a panic.

They heard a loud detonation above and astern of them.

"Target or End of Run, Oberleutnant?" asked Wassermann.

Consulting his stopwatch, Tröjer said, "Too soon for an End of Run, sir."

"Then pray it's the destroyer," said Wassermann. "Blow all ballast! Leutnant Mannstein, prepare to man the Flakvierling. Open fire as soon as we surface; aim for the bridge."

"Yes, sir," yelled Mannstein over the roar of the compressed air forcing the water out of the ballast tanks.

Roenneberg again started reciting the depth, "180 metres....170 metres....160 metres."

DARTMOUTH HAD JUST COME ABOUT and straightened for another attack, when the homing torpedo blew up against her propeller. The explosion peeled the stern back like a banana.

Mitchell was catapulted out of his chair to the deck, hitting his head on the compass binnacle as he went. He must have passed out for a moment because when he awoke, all was quiet except for the moaning of the injured. His head cleared and he was looking into the wide, unseeing eyes of Lieutenant Porter. Blood trickled out of the man's nose and mouth, and he was obviously dead.

Someone helped Mitchell to his chair. It was Lieutenant Blandford.

"Guns, how bad is it?" he asked. "Are we sinking?"

"I don't think so, sir," Blandford answered. "It looks like we lost most of the stern but the bulkheads appear to be holding. Thank God the depth charges in the racks weren't armed or they'd be exploding under us right now! We're still afloat, but I don't know for how long."

Somebody yelled, "U-boat surfacing dead ahead, 300 yards!"

"Guns," said Mitchell, clutching Blandford's sleeve, "take charge up forward. The gun is all we have left. Switch to H/E, and send Sub up here, if he's still alive."

"Yes, sir," said Blandford and left.

Sub-Lieutenant Martin soon arrived, bloodied but apparently not seriously hurt. Mitchell was just about to speak when a fusillade of 37mm shells hit the bridge. Most of it was above their heads but both ducked as the radio and radar aerials came down about them.

The 4" gun returned fire immediately but, having surfaced stern-on to Dartmouth, the U-boat was a very small target. The first shot was to port, the second to starboard; however, the third High Explosive shell found its mark. The firing from the U-boat ceased but, with the last discharge, so did the forward gun.

Martin picked up the bridge telephone, listened for a second, then turned to Mitchell. "Sir, a shell misfired and the casing is caught in the breech. They're trying to clear it but it's jammed in solid."

Oh God, thought Mitchell. Now we're helpless; we can't even call for help!

DARTMOUTH'S LAST SHOT had hit dead on the 37mm *Flak* gun abaft the Conning Tower, blowing both gun and gun crew overboard and spraying the bridge with shrapnel. Leutnant Mannstein was decapitated, his headless body falling to the deck. Wassermann was struck in the chest and arm but was able to hold himself upright with the aid of the search periscope housing.

U581 had surfaced only to find herself dead in the water, both diesel engines flooded and unable to start. The gun crew scrambled to the Wintergarten and opened fire in remarkable time. But now Wassermann stood alone, wounded, on a disabled boat, wondering why his opponent didn't just finish the job.

CHAPTER NINETEEN

THE SHRILL RING OF THE
TELEPHONE   interrupted   Tom
Garrett's reading once again. He
leaned over to pick it up, reaching for
his cup of coffee at the same time. He
lifted the receiver to his ear and
answered,   "Communications."
Bringing his coffee to his lips, he
listened for a second, then laid the cup
back down, untouched. "I'll pass it
along," was all he said. He replaced
the receiver, got up and ran down the
hall, headed for Lieutenant Ryan's
office.

Ryan was sitting at his desk reading
an action report of an aircraft attack
against a surfaced U-boat the day
before, north of the Virgin Rocks.
They'd   D/F'd   her   wireless

transmission at the Flemish Cap and, assuming she was headed west, had sent an air patrol out to intercept. The pilot claimed only damage but Ryan was more optimistic. The photographs taken by the observer showed the depth charges well inside lethal range. He looked up at the sound of running footsteps approaching.

His door burst open and Garrett came in. "Sir, U-boat attack in Conception Bay! I just got the word from Bell Island, two ships sunk!"

Ryan got up and went to his map. Looking at the pin he had repositioned a few hours earlier, he said, half to himself, "So, that's what you were up to. Son of a bitch!"

He turned around and, looking at Garrett, asked, "Any unauthorized transmissions out of the anchorage tonight?"

"Negative. Just the regular stuff," answered the Killick. "Somebody decided to recite a bedtime prayer, but that's about it."

"Okay, try and get one of the escorts, will you? I'll call the COS."

"Yes, sir," replied Garrett, and left.

Ryan picked up the phone, gave his name to the operator, and requested she contact Captain Harold Short, RCN, Chief-of-Staff, at home. He heard a click and then a sleepy voice say, "Short."

Ryan began, "Sorry to disturb you, sir. This is Lieutenant Ryan at ONI. We just got word that two ships have been sunk off Bell Island." He heard profanity at the other end, then the Captain asked him if he'd been in contact with *Dartmouth*.

"We're trying now, sir," said Ryan. He listened for a minute, scribbling notes on the pad in front of him. "Yes, sir, I'll call Commander Bloom right away." Ryan clicked the button on the phone, disconnecting it, then rang the operator. He exhaled loudly and when she answered, asked her to "Connect me to the Staff Officer (Operations), please." He waited. It was going to be a long night.

HMCS *DARTMOUTH* AND *U581* DRIFTED WITH THE TIDE, separated by 300 yards of still water - fortunately for *Dartmouth*, too close for a torpedo to arm, although a bow shot was iffy at the best of times. All was silent except for the wild hammering, and virulent profanity, coming from the 4" gun forward.

Dawn came and with it the notorious Newfoundland fog. Mitchell saw it rolling in from the mouth of Conception Bay like smoke, enveloping the two combatants. Slowly, each was lost from the other's view, and peace returned to this little part of the world.

Mitchell, now in his chair and fighting unconsciousness, asked Martin to tell Lieutenant Blandford to "forget the damn gun and prepare to abandon ship." He lost his battle to stay awake and, almost gratefully, slipped into the dark abyss.

CHAPTER TWENTY

KAPITÄN-LEUTNANT PETER SCHILLING SALUTED ADMIRAL DÖNITZ who bid him to sit down. *Kapitän* Gödt and *Kapitän-Leutnant* Hessler, who were present when Schilling arrived, also sat.

"How is your crew shaping up, *Kapitän-Leutnant?*" asked Dönitz.

"Well, sir. We are ready for our first war patrol," answered Schilling, somewhat anxiously.

He'd been surprised when Dönitz's Flag Lieutenant called him with the appointment. The Admiral often saw his boats off, especially for their first trip to the front, but it was the Flotilla Commander who briefed the captains on their orders, not the *Befehlshaber der U-Boote* himself.

"Peter, we're going to delay your patrol for a while. We have another job for you," began the Admiral. "We've lost three U-boats on weather reporting duty off Newfoundland over the past couple of months, all to aircraft. I've discontinued it for the time being, but only temporarily. We still need weather reports but the cost is getting too high. *Kapitän-Leutnant* Hessler has been working on a plan which, we hope, will kill two birds with one stone, so to speak."

"Günter, if you please." Dönitz looked at Hessler.

Hessler got up and walked to the wall map at the side. With a pencil he pointed to the area northwest of the Flemish Cap.

"The three boats were lost in this area, we understand all to aircraft. The nearest airfield is here, about five kilometres north of St. John's. We hope to neutralize it." Hessler looked at Schilling. Turning back to the map, he continued, "You will land a commando team here, at Middle Cove in Tor Bay, about four kilometres from the base. You are to remain offshore during the raid, then return to Middle Cove and pick them up. We estimate it will take them about one hour to travel overland and probably a bit more coming back. The actual attack should only take a half hour unless they run into trouble. The detonators will be delayed fuse so as not to alert the enemy until after you have picked up the team We are planning a couple of diversions to minimize the enemy forces in place, both offshore and at the base itself.

At the Admiral's inquiring look, he said, "Sir, I've been in contact with Admiral Canaris," referring to Admiral Wilhelm Canaris, head of the *Abwehr*, Germany's military intelligence service. "He told me that they have an operative in place in St. John's and some sort of civilian diversion can be initiated, a fire or something similar. This would draw off a lot of the base's manpower - firefighters, medical and off-duty personnel, etc., as well as those in St. John's itself.

At the Admiral's nod, he continued, "We are also going to have a couple of U-boats sending wireless transmissions further east to draw off Naval and Air Force assets. This should leave you unmolested while you wait for the commandos, as well as increase their chances of success.

"However, before you undertake this part of the plan, we want you to set up an automated weather station on the coast of Labrador.

Hessler again faced Dönitz, "Sir, I've chosen a location at the very tip of Labrador." With his pencil, he pointed to Cape Chidley on Labrador's northeast coast. "It's very remote, eliminating the chances of discovery, and has a clear field out to the Atlantic. I've spoken to Dr. Kurt Sömmermeyer, and both he and his technical assistant, Walter Hildebrandt, will accompany *U573* on her mission, to set up the station.

"This part of the plan will also allow the commando team to recover from the voyage, as well as practice disembarking from a U-boat in conditions similar to what they will encounter at Middle Cove.

Hessler finished, "The entire operation should take about three and a half weeks."

"Thank you, *Kapitän-Leutnant* Hessler," said Dönitz.

Looking back at Schilling, he continued. "*Kapitän-Leutnant*, you will disembark all your spare torpedoes and keep the ones already in their tubes for self-defence only. You will take the minimum number of crew necessary to operate your boat - no more - and stores for four weeks. *Kapitän-Leutnant* Hessler will go over all the details with you later." Dönitz concluded, "Any questions?"

Schilling answered, "Not right now, sir. I'd like to study the Op Plan first."

"Very good, *Kapitän-Leutnant*. Günter will accompany you down the hall to the Briefing Room and answer any questions."

The BdU stood up, followed by the others. Schilling saluted and left, trailed by Hessler. Dönitz sat down and, looking at Gödt, said, "Well, Eberhard, we'll see what happens."

"Yes, Admiral," replied Gödt.

CHAPTER TWENTY-ONE

MITCHELL FELT SOMEONE HOLD HIS HAND. He tried to open his eyes but the effort sent a bolt of pain through his temples. He tried again. It didn't hurt as much this time and, after blinking a few times, his vision cleared and he could see faces above him.

"Good morning, Sunshine!" It was Linda holding his hand. Behind her stood Commander Bloom.

"What...?" croaked Mitchell.

"You're in hospital in St. John's," explained Linda.

"My ship?"

"Tied up on the Southside," answered Bloom. "She'll need a new stern but that should only take a few months. But, I'm afraid she'll have to go to Halifax for that," he added, sneaking a quick look at Linda.

"How...?" started Mitchell.

"We got word of the attack from Bell Island. When we couldn't raise you, we dispatched HMCS *Chedabucto* to investigate. She found you about 0800 yesterday and towed you here."

"Yesterday?" said Mitchell.

"Yes, Lieutenant," said Bloom, "you've been unconscious since yesterday. Today's Monday, November 3."

"The U-boat?"

"Gone. Sunk or escaped, we don't know. A Digby bomber sighted a surfaced U-boat off Cape Race this morning but the fog closed in before it could attack. It might've been your sub."

A nurse came and said it was time to go. *Doctor's orders!* Bloom left, telling Mitchell he'd be back tomorrow with a Wren to get his report. Linda Halley stayed.

"I thought you had to go?" said Mitchell. "*Doctor's orders.*"

"I've got an in with the doctor," she smiled.

"Your father?"

"Uh-huh. He said you have a bad concussion and a couple of broken ribs but you'll live. It'll take a while before you're fit for command again, I'm afraid, but he says all you need is tender, loving care." She raised her eyebrows, "The tender loving I can supply; he can look after the care."

Mitchell squeezed her hand. "Linda, marry me?"

"Yes," she said without hesitation, and kissed him. "Now, rest please, Lieutenant Mitchell."

"Yes, ma'am," he said and, smiling, closed his eyes. Linda stayed, holding his hand until he fell asleep.

CHAPTER TWENTY-TWO

ROGUES BATISTE FINISHED THE WELD on *U573*'s starboard saddle tank and leaned back to admire his handiwork. Perfect, he thought. But it wasn't. Batiste had used an old welding rod to fill the seam, then torched it over to give the appearance of a proper job. It would split at the first bit of heavy weather or jar of a depth charge attack, allowing the air to escape from the ballast tank. Not enough to sink the U-boat but certainly adequate to cause problems, especially if combined with other weather or battle damage.

Batiste's was just one of a hundred little acts of sabotage perpetrated against the *Kriegsmarine* every day since France was occupied in 1940.

They'd increased in scope and frequency as the war progressed and the Germans went on the defensive. So too, did the brutality of the reprisals. But Batiste was safe for now; the Germans hadn't started recording the names of the *yardies* working on particular U-boats, yet. But they would soon.

Batiste looked across the harbour at the impregnable *Keromann* U-boat bunker. Why the British had not bombed it while it was under construction was beyond him. Now it was too late, and the boats inside were untouchable. He'd told them, and continued to tell them, as construction progressed but they preferred to go after the U-boats under repair alongside instead. Soft targets. A mistake.

Batiste lit a cigarette and enjoyed the warm rays of the morning sun. Despite being early November, there were still some nice days left. He looked with interest at the comings and goings on board the U-boat he was working on. It was new, fresh in from

Germany, but there seemed to be an awful lot of activity aboard it this morning - strange activity. They'd unloaded all the spare torpedoes earlier that morning and there had been a lot of hammering and banging up forward in what had to be the torpedo room.

Just then, two large trucks pulled up alongside and a dozen cammo-fatigued commandos disembarked and stood at parade rest on the quay. The tailgate of the second truck banged down and waiting matelots started transferring crates of equipment from the truck to the U-boat. Workmen exited from the forward hatch, and in single file, the commandos strode on board, followed by two other men in civilian clothes and carrying suitcases.

The work detail foreman called over to Batiste to come up if he was finished and get on with the next job. Batiste swore at him under his breath, gathered up his torch and kitbag, and climbed up the ladder.

The U-boat's skipper arrived in a staff limousine, an unusual occurrence, accompanied by what looked like the Admiral in charge of U-boats, Dönitz. The two men shook hands outside the car and the junior officer saluted. He marched down the prow to the deck of the U-boat and accepted a salute from one of the boat's officers, then turned and addressed the crew lined up along the afterdeck.

The Captain finished his speech, none of which Batiste understood, climbed up the Conning Tower ladder to the bridge, and disappeared below as the rest of the crew dispersed. The water alongside churned. The U-boat separated from the quay and, led by a minesweeper, headed out into the Bay of Biscay, just as the skipper reappeared on the bridge in his scuffed white commander's hat and oil-stain leather sea coat.

This was very curious, thought Batiste. I must get it off to the British tonight. Rogues Batiste did more than just commit petty acts of sabotage; he was also a major source of intelligence for the British. He had a small, but fairly powerful, wireless secreted in his bedroom at the boarding house in town, and regularly sent signals to London on anything he thought might be useful.

Even incidental stuff was included - who was awarded what decoration, in a fight, promoted, which Flotilla won the soccer game, and so on. This information was used by the British for their *Atlantiksender*, the Black Propaganda station which tried to undermine morale in the German *Ubootewaffe* by extraordinarily knowing broadcasts. Listening to it was *verboten,* of course, but many U-boatmen did anyway, as they considered it more accurate in its reporting than the home stations. It also played better music!

At day's end, Batiste punched out and walked through the front gate, past the armed sentries, to where his bicycle was chained to the security fence. He headed off down the street, turning right at *Rue Maréchal Foch,* then taking a left at *Blvd deCastelnau*, just past *Les Trois*

Soeurs. The club was one of the *Ubootewaffe*'s favourite off-duty haunts in Lorient (that and the bar at the *Hotel Beau Sejour*) and Batiste worked there part-time.

He arrived at his boarding house and, hoisting his bike up on one shoulder, entered the vestibule. He'd just deposited it against the wall with those of the other boarders when his landlady, *Madame* Gérard, opened the inner door.

"*Bonne soirée*, Rogues," she said. "Good day at work?"

"*Oui, Madame*," replied Batiste.

"Anything interesting happen?"

"No, just the regular stuff."

"*Bon*," said *Madame* Gérard. "Well, see you later, Rogues. I'm just going down to the *patisserie* to get some bread to go with supper. I shouldn't be long."

"Okay, *Madame*. See you then," said Batiste.

Madame Gérard trundled on down the road while Batiste mounted the stairs, several at a time, until reaching his third floor room. The other boarders shared their rooms, but Batiste paid extra for the privacy, complaining of insomnia. He had about fifteen minutes, so he had to hurry. He unlocked the door, entered and relocked it behind him. He dug his transmitter out from underneath his clothes in the closet, connected the battery and strung the aerial while the transmitter warmed up. By the time he'd finished, the radio was ready. He tapped out his signal, got the acknowledgement, then dismantled the set and packed it away. The entire operation took less than ten minutes.

He'd just finished getting washed in the bathroom adjacent to his room when he heard *Madame* Gérard open the front door. He went back to his room and waited to be called for supper. Later, he would go to *Les Trois Soeurs* and see what other tidbits he could pick up for the *Atlantiksender*.

CHAPTER TWENTY-THREE

LIEUTENANT FRANK RYAN SAT
IN HIS OFFICE reading the action
report he'd taken from Lieutenant
Alistair Mitchell, skipper of HMCS
Dartmouth, the day before.

It sounded like quite an experience -
a firefight, losing his stern to what
sounded like an acoustic torpedo, all in
Conception Bay, ten minutes from St.
John's as the crow flies. The homing
torpedo was a new, disturbing
development. He'd have to get more on
that from the young lieutenant.

The report concluded with the total
number of Allied lives lost. Including
the forty from the torpedoed ore
carriers and the ten killed on the
corvette, there were fifty. It was a
damn shame *Dartmouth*'s First

Lieutenant was killed. They really needed experienced, seagoing officers to command the steady stream of escorts coming down the ways.

Mitchell was still in hospital, and would be for a few days yet. Commander Bloom asked Ryan to interview Mitchell, and he and the cute little Wren down the hall at Headquarters had gone. When they'd arrived, that pretty Second Officer from Operations was there. Mitchell introduced her as Linda Halley, his fiancée.

They'd talked at length about the action itself but also Mitchell's impressions of the German skipper and his tactics - Ryan's reporter instincts humming. Mitchell was very informative and detailed; nothing was too small to mention. He asked about the U-boat, and Ryan confirmed that it had gotten away. They'd found the sub's *Flak* gun with grappling hooks on the bottom of Conception Bay and brought it up, but no other evidence to suggest that the U-boat was also on the bottom. Mitchell wanted to know about his ship and crew, and was visibly upset at the number of casualties.

Linda Halley stayed the whole time. As she worked in Operations, Ryan figured it was okay; Linda would see the report eventually anyway. When he'd finished the interview, she'd touched Ryan's arm and indicated with her eyes that she wanted to talk to him outside. He bid good-bye to Mitchell, who was half asleep by this time anyway, and left. Linda Halley followed him out. The cute little Wren from down the hall waited a polite distance away, shooting daggers at Linda.

"Is he in any kind of trouble?" she asked, ignoring the other woman.

"Not that I'm aware of. As a matter of fact, I've heard rumblings that he's going to be promoted. Why?"

"I'm afraid they'll try to pin this mess on Alistair."

"Oh, I wouldn't worry." Ryan lifted the pages in his hand. "To me, it looks like he went by the book. Now, the higher-ups will probably find fault, they usually do. If Mitch had sunk the bastard on his way into Conception Bay, they'd say he'd used too many depth charges. But the Old Man will back him up. Commodore Taylor can play hard ball, too, when he wants to. Mitch'll be all right."

"Good. Thank you," Linda said gratefully.

"Look, Miss Halley...," started Ryan.

"Linda, please, Lieutenant," interrupted the girl.

"Linda. You can call me Frank. Linda, do you think it would be okay if I touched base with Mitch from time to time while he's recovering? Unofficially, of course."

"I can't see why not," answered Linda.

Ryan continued, "I'm basically a landlubber, and there are times when I really need to run something past an experienced, seagoing officer in utmost confidence. You know the bunch in Ops, most of them, their sea time has been on sailboats in the summer. I need someone who's been in the thick of things - who's dealt with the U-boats first hand. Mitch might pick up on something I wouldn't, some clue that might put it all together."

"Sure. I think he'd be happy to. Alistair will be staying at my place when he gets out." With a quick glance at the other Wren, she quickly added, "With me and my father   And housekeeper."

"Linda, it's none of my business," Ryan said with a smiled.

Blushing, Linda dug through her handbag for a pen and a piece of paper. She found them, scribbled her number and gave it to Ryan. "Alistair should be out by Friday."

"Thanks," said Ryan. He shook her hand, and he and his Wren sidekick headed for the stairs.

THERE WAS A KNOCK ON HIS DOOR and Garrett entered. Ryan looked up from his reading and the Killick said, "Something from the British, sir. Relayed by Naval Service Headquarters."

"Fine, put it there, will you?" said Ryan, nodding to the stack of papers on the corner of his desk.

"You might like to read this now, sir."

"Why?" asked Ryan, reaching out to take the message from Garrett.

"It's about a U-boat that left France a couple of days ago, without her full load of torpedoes but with a squad of what looked like commandos on board."

"So why send it to us?"

Garrett handed him another signal, "Because they D/F'd her southeast of Greenland this morning. She's headed our way."

"Do they know where she's going?"

"It doesn't say, sir," said Garrett.

"Thanks, Tom." Garrett nodded and left. Ryan looked at the map on the wall. They'll D/F the sub again when she passes Cape Farewell, he thought. And then she'll join the other red pins sticking in the map. Until then, he would just have to wait.

CHAPTER TWENTY-FOUR

U573 PLOWED THROUGH THE
TWENTY-FOOT SEAS, heaving and
plunging as she fought against 60-
knot headwinds. Schilling had taken
only the most senior members of his
crew, plus all the officers. They were
used to this kind of weather, but the
commandos, well, they weren't doing
so well. Most were seasick, and the
bow compartment didn't smell very
good. The squad's commander,
Heydemann, was okay. A career
officer and a veteran of France and the
Norway invasion, he'd lived through
worse than this, but most of his men
were younger and less seasoned.

Schilling's crew took pity on the
commandos, giving them dry bread
and bicarbonate soda to help settle

their stomachs, but most of them just wanted to die. Dr. Sömmermeyer and his assistant, who were assigned to the Petty Officer's quarters, hadn't left their bunks since crossing the Bay of Biscay.

The bad weather also eliminated the chance of getting a good star sighting and they were running on *Dead Reckoning* only. Somewhere north of them - who knew how far - was Cape Farewell, on Greenland's southern tip. Added to this, the starboard saddle tank was leaking again, necessitating running the low pressure blowers continually to maintain trim while on the surface. *U573*'s First Watch Officer, *Oberleutnant* Werner von Blücher, was driven to distraction by it all.

The bridge hatch banged open, and *Hauptmann* Karl Heydemann asked permission to come up.

"Granted," said Schilling.

Heydemann was dressed in foul weather gear, as were all the men on watch. He climbed through the oval hatch, banging it shut once he was through. With little chance of an air attack, it was better to keep the hatch closed rather than risk an electrical short below in the *Zentrale*. A wave exploded at the base of the Conning Tower, filling the horseshoe-shaped bridge with the cold Atlantic before sluicing aft through the *Wintergarten.*

"*Gott in Himmel*!" swore the tall commando officer. "What weather!"

"We've been in worse," answered Schilling. "How are your men holding up?"

"Oh, they'll survive. But we might have some trouble getting them back aboard after the mission. At least with the enemy you can fight back, eh?"

"True enough," said the U-boat skipper, sympathetically.

Heydemann was what most people pictured a hardened commando to look like. Tall, well-built, close cropped blond hair. He even had a scar under one eye. A duelling mishap? wondered Schilling. Heydemann had refused Schilling's offer of a bunk in the Wardroom, preferring to sleep up forward with his men.

"How long do you think this will last?" asked Heydemann.

"No idea," replied Schilling. "That's why the weather station is so important. Weather travels West to East in the Northern Hemisphere. So, if there's a storm off Newfoundland, it will hit the mid-Atlantic in a day or so, depending on how fast it's going. You can imagine trying to attack a convoy in this!"

Just then, a gigantic wave hit the U-boat. All were swept off their feet, and the boat heeled dangerously to port. Submerged, their lungs screaming for air, the men heard a tremendous banging and rendering aft. When the water subsided, and the bridge watch coughed and gasped for air, one of the lookouts yelled, "*Kaleu*, the gun!"

All looked to the *Wintergarten* and, where the 37mm *Flak* gun used to be, only a gaping hole in the grating remained.

"I think it's time to pull the plug, Captain," said Schilling.

"You'll get no argument from me, Commander," yelled Heydemann, over the wind.

At Schilling's command, the lookouts jumped down the hatch, followed by Heydemann and finally the skipper, who dogged it closed as he went. *U573* quickly settled and, with the next wave, disappeared from view.

IT WAS A COLD, BLUSTERY AFTERNOON and Linda buttoned Mitchell's coat up before easing him out of the back seat of the taxi. The driver passed her his carry-all, and she took Mitchell's elbow and started up the steps to the front door. Mrs. O'Brien was waiting with it opened and took Mitchell's bag from Linda as they entered. Linda helped him shrug out of his mackintosh and gave it to the housekeeper.

Mitchell held on to the banister and gingerly mounted the stairs, one by one, waving off Linda's attempt at assistance. They reached the top hall, and Linda went ahead and opened the door to a bedroom. It was the same one Mitchell stayed in before, and there was a fire burning in the small grate. He felt as if he had come home.

Linda carefully helped him out of his jacket, tie and shirt. She pulled a pyjama top over his head before helping him haul off his trousers. He lay down on the four poster bed and Linda pulled up the covers, gently kissing his forehead.

"Ribs hurt?"

"Like the devil," he gasped, and Linda said, "Tender loving care is all you need. Now, go to sleep. You looked pooped."

Mitchell smiled and snuggled further down under the covers. He was soon asleep and Linda left. The afternoon turned to evening, and then to night. Still Alistair Mitchell slept.

MITCHELL AWOKE AND SAW A SHADOW by his door. As it approached the still smouldering, hours-old fire, he recognized Linda. She was wearing her flannel nightgown but, as she got closer, she dropped it to the floor. He slid awkwardly over to the side of the bed and lifted the covers. She climbed in next to him and gently put her fingers to his lips as he started to say something.

"I almost lost you," was all she said.

LEADING SEAMAN GARRETT ENTERED FRANK RYAN'S OFFICE with another signal in his hand. He passed it to Ryan, saying, "They've D/F'd that sub, sir. He's about 200 miles southwest of Cape Farewell. I've just checked with Meteorology, weather's too bad to send a patrol plane."

"We got a number on this one yet?" asked Ryan.

"Yes, sir. *U573*," answered Garrett.

"All right! Keep me posted."

Garrett exited as Ryan got up from his desk and went over to his wall map. He took a pin from the wooden frame and stuck it into the map at the position indicated in the signal. What are you up to? Maybe he would have to pay a call on Lieutenant Mitchell sooner than he had thought.

CHAPTER TWENTY-FIVE

ONE OF THE TRULY UNIQUE
FEATURES of the port of St. John's,
Newfoundland, is the swift transition
from the inhospitable North Atlantic
to the calmer waters of the harbour.
Just like Captain Nemo's volcanic
hideaway in *20,000 Leagues Under
The Sea*, once through the secret
portal - The Narrows can only be seen
when faced dead-on - the storm-
battered sailor finds sanctuary. It has
always amazed mariners, right from
when St. John's was just a summer
anchorage and the Fishing Admirals
were the law.

The reason for this phenomenon is
the Southside Hills, stretching from
the harbour entrance all the way to
the fishing village of Petty Harbour,

ten miles south. The Hills form a solid wall protecting the low-lying areas inshore from the savage gales that come in from the world's stormiest ocean.

The Southside Hills were also important militarily. Both the British and the French swooped down from them at various times over a hundred year period, to capture St. John's in a see-saw battle for possession. It finally ended with a British victory. Since that time, the Southside Hills and their sister, Signal Hill, have protected the City from both the elements and would-be marauders, including pirates and privateers.

With the arrival of the Royal Canadian Navy in 1941, the Southside Hills were again of strategic importance. Concrete gun emplacements were built on Signal Hill and at old Fort Amherst to guard the entrance to the Harbour. And a naval base, complete with barracks, grew to eventually encompass the entire south side of St. John's Harbour from the Narrows to the new Royal

Canadian Navy Dockyard. As a result, the region east of Job's Bridge Crossing was off limits to all but military personnel. However, the area south, from Blackhead Road, was open to all and full of great fishing and swimming holes, as well as hiking trails and picnic spots.

Kilbride, and in particular Petty Harbour Road, was very popular. During the summer months most of the young people in the vicinity, especially the boys, spent every fine day of the holidays trouting or swimming in the numerous ponds, or hiking along the many trails, some of which went all the way to Petty Harbour.

Adults also frequented the locale. Many went up in the evenings after work, to get in a couple of hours fishing before the sun set. It was a common sight to see cars and trucks parked at the top of the gravel road where their owners had left them to walk to a favourite fishing spot.

But not in late November!

That's why Peter and Billy Murphy, cousins, were surprised to see the black Ford pull into the woods at the top of Petty Harbour Road. Being from Kilbride, and only thirteen years old, they went up into the woods often, even in the fall and winter, to explore or exchange daydreams. They even had a secret hideaway built out of bits and pieces of scrap wood they'd collected all summer. But it was strange to see a car up here this late in the year.

"What d'ya suppose he's doing?" said Peter, as they continued up the road.

"I dunno, maybe goin' for a walk?"

"Then why park in the woods? Most people just park on the road."

Billy just shrugged, not being terribly interested. As they neared the spot where the car had pulled in, they heard a door slam and when they reached the clearing, saw a man disappear down a path. In his hand was a steel fishing rod. The cousins looked at each other and, with the naivety of a thirteen-year-old, Billy said, "He's goin' fishing. We'd better go and tell 'im the season's over."

"Yeah," said Peter, equally as naive. "He could get into a lot of trouble if the Constable catches him."

The two boys trotted down the path after the man, but within five minutes realized they must have passed him, and headed back. As they came to a large, fallen tree, they heard a strange sound - an irregular series of *beeps*, a pause, then more *beeps*. Peter and Billy stopped in their tracks. They knew from Boy Scouts that the *beeps* were Morse Code and, despite only being in their early teens, both had been exposed to the many wartime posters proclaiming *Loose Lips Sink Ships* and *There Are Spies Amongst Us*. And of course, *The Shadow* was always catching Nazi agents on his weekly radio program.

Peter whispered, "He's a spy."

Now the two cousins were scared, really scared. They backed slowly and quietly into the woods, afraid flight would alert the man on the other side of the fallen tree. They crouched down behind some bushes and waited for him to finish.

Shortly he did and, when he reappeared, the boys could clearly see what they'd thought was a fishing rod. An antenna! The man was wearing a wide-brimmed hat but they saw he had jet black hair and a dark complexion. He ran back up the path, and the two boys stayed immobile until they heard the car door slam and the engine catch. Only as the sound faded in the distance did they cautiously leave their hiding place.

Peter and Billy crossed the path and hopped over the tree. On the ground, covered with cut boughs and tree moss, the boys discovered a green tarpaulin. After pushing off the camouflage, they pulled up the tarp. Underneath were two wooden suitcases. One contained two car batteries, a rare commodity in wartime St. John's, and the other, a radio, complete with earphones and a built-in transmitting key.

And on the underside of each cover was the Nazi eagle and swastika!

U573 NOSED HER BOWS into the
Bay, near silent on her electric motors.
She didn't need to, no one would hear
her if she roared in with both diesels
at Full. But, this was supposed to be a
dry run for the landing at Middle
Cove.

They sighted Cape Chidley at
midday, much to the relief of all. They
hadn't had a proper star sight in five
days. Working south, Schilling
searched for a suitable landing site.
Using the echo sounder, he eased the
U-boat between Home Island and the
Avayalik Islands, finally rounding the
southern tip of the Hutton Peninsula.

Schilling finally found an agreeable
spot in what the chart called
Attinaukjuke Bay, but Schilling
waited until nightfall for the run in -
again to duplicate conditions for the
attack on Torbay Air Base. It was now
1845 hours, and the U-boat anchored
approximately 300 metres off the
beach.

The forward hatch opened and two shadows emerged. Behind them followed three clumsy bundles. These were unwrapped by the two on deck and inflated. Quiet orders brought forth more men, who helped launch the rubber boats. All six jumped in, a pair in each, clutching the casing to prevent them from drifting. More shadows appeared, and equipment was passed from the open hatch to the boats. Soon they were loaded, and the remaining commandos, plus the two civilians, boarded.

With swift synchronized strokes, the three rafts devoured the 300 metres and reached the shore. Automatic weapons were removed from watertight wrappings, and two men fanned out from the landing area, taking positions about 100 metres from the water's edge. The remainder unloaded the boats and, with the civilians at the tail end followed by two sentries, headed into the bush.

The trek continued for about half an hour, by which time the two scientists were gasping for breath. They came to a barren area and *Hauptmann* Heydemann raised his arm, halting the troop. With hand signals, he indicated to those behind that this was the spot. The commandos unshouldered their heavy loads and the assembly began.

Back at the U-boat, repairs were underway. The torn grating of the *Wintergarten* was planked over and the leaking weld in the saddletank sealed with concrete. The boat was ventilated, and refuse thrown overboard in weighted sacks. The diesel engines were started, and the batteries fully charged. Schilling sent two armed petty officers ashore in the U-boat's dingy to guard the rubber boats and prevent a surprise attack from shore, just in case. Dawn found the *U573* alert, but with many of the crew sleeping off the night's labours.

Ashore, work progressed uninterrupted, and finally at 1800, less than twenty-four hours after anchoring, the clandestine installation was ready. Dr. Sömmermeyer hit the switch and Weather Station *Kurt* started broadcasting. They threw a few empty cigarette packages and matchboxes around, and started the trip back to the *U573*, dragging two evergreen trees behind them to cover their tracks in the snow. They arrived back on board at 1830. At 2240, now with the sentries aboard, the U-boat weighed anchor and left the Bay at full speed. Just offshore, a short signal was sent confirming that the first part of the mission had been completed successfully.

Shortly thereafter, the message was in Dönitz's hand. He smiled and passed it to Eberhard Gödt.

AT THE SAME TIME, Seaman Garrett passed it to Lieutenant Frank Ryan, who had just come on duty. "Now, why the hell would he go all the way up there?" he said, looking at Garrett, of course not knowing the contents of the signal, just its point of origin.

"Damned if I know, sir. There's nothing up there, 'cept maybe a bunch

of Eskimos, and they don't even know
there's a war on!"

"Tom, ask Goose (Bay Air Station)
to send a patrol plane up there to
investigate, would you? Something on
skis so they can land, just in case they
find anything. I'll clear it with
Tommy," said Ryan, referring to the
Staff Officer (Intelligence) and picked
up the phone. Ryan's immediate
superior was Commander Miles
"Tommy" Thomas, RCNR. It was still
relatively early so Ryan didn't mind
calling. Thomas' housekeeper
answered the phone. Ryan identified
himself and asked to speak to the
Commander. He glanced up at Garrett
standing in the doorway.

"Thomas."

"Sir, this is Lieutenant Frank Ryan.
That U-boat full of commandos we've
been tracking for the past ten days,
we've just D/F'd it off northern
Labrador. I want to send a plane up to
investigate."

"What do you suspect, Lieutenant?"
asked Thomas.

"I don't really know, Commander," said Ryan. "There's nothing up there worth a landing party. Certainly not with commandos. That in itself makes it very suspicious."

"Okay, go ahead. Keep me advised." Thomas rung off.

Ryan hung up the phone and said to Garrett, "Do it."

Garrett departed. Ryan got up and went to his wall map. He took the pin from south of Greenland and placed it off northern Labrador. He sat back down and started to think about why a U-boat was where it had no reason to be. He was still pondering the question when he left the next morning at the end of his shift.

THE RCAF C-64 NORSEMAN lifted off from Goose Bay Air Station and climbed to 5,000 feet, making a wide arc north. At the controls sat Flying Officer Pat Brown, "Poppy" to his friends due to his advanced age and weathered features. Poppy was an old-time bush pilot with thousands of hours of *seat of the pants* flying in northern Ontario - hence his posting to *Air Reconnaissance and Supply* at Goose Bay.

His Norseman, which Brown affectionately called "the Beast", was a workhorse of an aircraft. Weighing 7,200 pounds, she was powered by a 650 horsepower Pratt & Whitney radial engine that gave her a cruising speed of 134 knots per hour. She carried two crew plus seven passengers, or equivalent dead weight, and was a bitch to get off the ground fully loaded. But after you did, you couldn't ask for a smoother flying, more reliable airplane.

This morning, Brown was hungover like a bear, the result of a night at the *Officers' Club* on the American side of the air base. Isolated as it was, and with the neighbouring communities of Happy Valley and Mud Lake off limits to military personnel, there wasn't much else to do in Goose Bay other than drink. And play pool. And, of course, the Americans had the best of both. So, Poppy and most of his cohorts spent their off-duty hours with their Yank neighbours.

Seated next to Brown, Leading Aircraftman Tom Dunne, the Norseman's Flight Engineer, Wireless Operator, Navigator (and Stewardess! proclaimed Poppy to all and sundry) unscrewed the cap of a thermos of coffee. He poured a cup and passed it to his boss, along with a couple of aspirins. Brown mumbled his thanks, popped the pills and gulped down a mouthful of coffee. Dunne replaced the cap and poked the thermos under his seat. Twenty years old and a Pentecostal, the young man drank neither liquor nor coffee. And felt it was his God-given mission to reform Poppy Brown's evil ways. He hadn't been too successful to date, but at least he kept Brown flying, and out of the guardhouse. Poppy called him "Mother".

"What's the mission this morning, Poppy?" Dunne asked cheerfully. He knew damn well what the mission was, he just wanted Poppy awake and reasonably alert.

"Some darn fool thing," growled Brown. "They D/F'd a U-boat transmission off Martin Bay the other night, and St. John's wants us to take a look."

"Wouldn't a Hudson or Catalina be better for that? I mean, even if we find the sub, we can't do anything."

"Naw. They don't want us to find it," answered Brown, sarcastically, "just see if it landed anything."

"Landed anything!" Dunne consulted the map on his knees. "Why would a sub land anything way up there?"

"Damned if I know, Mother," grumbled Brown.

They followed the coastline for the next two and a half hours. Visibility was good and they could see the snow-covered cliffs below with ease.

Finally, Dunne announced, "We're there, Poppy."

Brown throttled back the engine and started a gentle spiral downward, levelling off at 1,000 feet.

"What are we looking for?" asked Dunne.

"I dunno," said Brown, "a camp, people...anything!"

They flew a box search for the next twenty minutes, Dunne scanning the ground with his binoculars.

Suddenly, he stiffened. "Got something, Poppy!"

"Whereaway, Mother?"

"There," said Dunne, pointing below. "About 5 o'clock."

Brown banked the Norseman to starboard and, mimicking the RAF - who he actually didn't particularly like - said, "*Tally Ho*, chaps!"

FRANK RYAN WALKED DOWN THE HALL to his office, wishing those he met, "Good evening." Garrett was waiting for him, and Ryan saw he had a signal in each hand. He hung up his coat and asked, "What have we got?"

Garrett said, "Do you want the bad news first or the worst?"

"Bad first."

"The patrol didn't find much, just an automated weather station."

"Ours or theirs?"

"Ours."

"Sure?"

"Yup. Marked *Canadian Weather Service*. There were even empty American cigarette packs and match boxes around."

"Damn! What else?"

"*U573*'s heading south. They D/F'd her a little while ago off St. Anthony."

"So, she's not going home."

"Nope."

"Then where's she going?"

"No idea."

"Okay. Thanks," said Ryan. Garrett left.

Ryan got up to move the pin on the map. He noticed there were more than when he'd left that morning. All south of St. John's. "What the hell is going on?" he said aloud. He lit a cigarette and left his office, headed for the combined RCN/RCAF Operations Room.

When he got there, all was quiet. With no important convoys passing through the Command's area or any major anti-submarine operations currently underway, only the minimum number of staff was required. If anything happened, all could be called back to duty very quickly. Now, only the Night Duty Officer, a pompous Royal Navy lieutenant, a few Wrens, and a Leading Air Woman or two were minding the plot. Ryan went over to the full wall map at his right. Off St. John's and along the southeast Avalon were a half dozen U-boat markers.

He felt a hand at his elbow. It was Linda Halley. "Hi, Linda," he said, turning. "When did all this start?" He nodded to the map.

"About lunchtime. Since then, they've been popping up all over the place."

"Heading south?" asked Ryan.

"No. We'd D/F one off St. John's, then an hour later, another down by Bay Bulls. Then, two hours later, there's one out on the Grand Banks. It's been like that all day. We've dispatched patrols but it seems like the U-boats send and then dive. By the time the plane gets there, they're gone."

"That's really strange. Usually, they lay low during the day and do their chatting at night." He paused. "Gathering for a kill?" wondered Ryan.

"Nothing to kill," replied Linda. "The regular coastal convoys – really, small change," she said. "Nothing worth this type of concentration."

Ryan indicated the marker off St. Anthony. "That one's another real mystery. You've read the signals. What do you think he's doing?"

"Joining the others?"

"Could be. But if so, why the commandos?"

Linda Halley shrugged. Ryan asked her about Mitchell.

"Fine," she said. "He's at home now."

Ryan noted her use of the more familiar term rather than just 'my place'. "Would it be okay for me to talk to him tomorrow, maybe after supper? Or are you two going to the dance at the Knights of Columbus?"

"No. I'm on duty and Alistair's still down about Lieutenant Porter. But he would probably welcome the company," she answered.

"Great," said Ryan, "about seven?"

"Sure. I won't be home but Mrs. O'Brien will let you in. She treats Alistair like gold. Every time he turns around she's asking him if he'd like a cup of tea. And he's too polite to say no! He complains that he keeps having to pee like a racehorse," she said with a chuckle.

"Nice lady."

"Yes, she is," said Linda, remembering.

"Okay," said Ryan. "Tell Mitch I'll be by. See you." Linda waved and he returned to his office.

RYAN SAT AT HIS DESK, lit a cigarette, and reviewed everything he knew so far. They had a boatload of commandos heading towards them, after a slight detour of several hundred miles to northern Labrador; a weather station; and a pack of U-boats forming up on the Grand Banks. What did it all mean?

Well, first off, let's check on that weather station. He picked up the phone directory on his desk and, under the Cs, started looking for the *Canadian Weather Service*. Not there. Okay, let's try *Weather Service*. Not there either. All right, maybe it's military. He checked that directory and couldn't find it there either. Geez, what is going on? he thought, exasperated. He picked up the phone and dialled Lieutenant Bill Bennett RCNVR at Meteorology.

"Lieutenant Bennett."

"Hi, Bill. It's Frank down the hall."

"Hi, Frank," replied Bennett. "What can I do for Naval Intelligence? Now, isn't that a contradiction of terms," he joked.

"Very funny, Bill," answered Ryan. "I'm trying to get a number for the *Canadian Weather Service* but can't find it."

"That's because it doesn't exist."

"What do you mean it doesn't exist? They've got a weather station up in northern Labrador," said Ryan.

"There could be, but it would have to be military, or the *National Weather Service's*. There is no *Canadian*

Weather Service. But, why the hell would anyone need one way up there anyway? Both of us have a weather office at every airport or air base in Canada and Newfoundland, including Labrador. It doesn't rain without us knowing it!"

"I see. Well, thanks, Bill."

"My pleasure."

Ryan hung up the phone and dug out the report from Goose Bay. Yes, they definitely said *Canadian Weather Service*, not *National*. He added that to his list.

U573 WAS ON THE SURFACE, travelling at her maximum speed of 18 knots. Considering the short duration of the patrol, she had fuel to waste. And little time to spare. They had to be at Middle Cove by the following night. So the closer they were before diving at dawn, the better. They'd surfaced a couple of hours before, sent a position report, and headed southeast, hell-bent for leather. *Oberleutnant* von Blücher had the bridge watch and Schilling was in the wardroom with *Hauptmann* Heydemann.

"We should reach Middle Cove by 2100 tomorrow," said Schilling. "We'll reconnoitre it, then surface at 2200 and head in. I'll try to get as close to shore as I can but the chart shows it shelves pretty quickly."

"Very good," said Heydemann. "All the aircraft should be on night patrol or refuelling. How are they going to get rid of the base personnel?"

"Fire or something in town. Whatever it is, it will start around 2200. So, by the time you commence the raid, the base should be almost deserted."

"I hope so. Twelve men against a whole air base aren't good odds!" replied Heydemann. Schilling nodded and called out into the passageway for *Smuti* to put on another pot of coffee. They could sleep when they submerged at first light. Now, they needed to go over every detail.

CHAPTER TWENTY-SIX

U656 SURFACED FOR THE
SIXTH TIME since sunrise. She had
been all over the southern Grand
Banks and was now off Cape Race at
the southern tip of the Avalon
Peninsula. *Kapitän-Leutnant* Ernst
Kröning climbed through the hatch to
the bridge. The sun was bright and
the captain and lookouts were
momentarily blinded by its intensity.

Ensign William Tepuni, USN, of
VP-82, flying a Lockheed Hudson out
of Argentia Naval/Air Station, did a
double-take as the U-boat surfaced
just off his starboard wing tip. Acting
fast to maintain surprise, he banked
the aircraft and came at the
submarine out of the sun. He released
two depth charges 'by eye' and happily

saw geysers erupt on either side of the U-boat, straddling her.

As he came around for another run, he noted that the stern was awash and men were jumping off the Conning Tower into the water. The bow slid under, suction taking the few survivors down with it. Bubbles of oil continued to come to the surface for the next twenty minutes as Tepuni circled. Finally, fuel getting low, he departed. The oil slick drifted south with the current, the only marker on the grave of *Kapitän-Leutnant* Kröning and his entire crew.

LIEUTENANT ALISTAIR MITCHELL sat in a high-backed chair by the fire, looking into the flames. He'd just finished supper and Linda had left earlier to start her shift at Operations. He smoked a cigarette and sipped his tea, almost afraid Mrs. O'Brien wouldcome in to see if he wanted another. He was tea'd out, and just the thought made him want to take a piss!

He thought of John Porter. His body had been sent back to Porter's hometown of London, Ontario, a few days ago. Mitchell had included with the personal effects, a short note of condolence to his family. It was formal and proper, and just words.

Mitchell had wanted to tell them what a friend Porter had been; how he had kept Mitchell sane out in the North Atlantic when ships were exploding and men were dying. Most of all, he wanted to tell them what a waste it all was - the death, the suffering, the destruction. All because of one man's dreams of conquest and racial superiority!

The doorbell rang but Mitchell hardly noticed. He heard voices, recognizing one as the housekeeper's, the other was male. Probably looking for the Doctor. He heard Mrs. O'Brien say, "Right in there, Lieutenant," and stood up as Frank Ryan entered.

Ryan extended his hand and Mitchell shook it. The Intelligence Officer asked how Mitchell was feeling.

"Okay, I guess," said Mitchell. "My ribs still hurt and I have a heck of a dent on the side of my head, but at least I'm alive, I suppose."

"Look, Mitch," said Ryan, "you did the best you could. It's war, after all, and people unfortunately get killed." Survivor's guilt, thought Ryan. Why did he survive and others didn't?

"Not a half mile offshore!"

"Sure they do. Think of the slaughter along the American eastern seaboard. Ships being torpedoed right off the beach. And the Yanks still didn't have the sense to turn off the lights ashore. Would hurt tourism, they said. Mitch, it is not your bloody fault!"

"I wish I was as convinced of my innocence as you are. I just don't know anymore."

Ryan asked, "Did you get the verdict from the Board of Inquiry yet?"

"Yes."

"And?"

"And they found my judgement wanting."

"They would! Especially the Royal Navy types. The Brits think they have all the answers," said Ryan, thinking specifically of Lieutenant Lewis-Smythe RN at Operations.

Mitchell raised an eyebrow at that, but continued. "They thought I should have set up the patrol pattern better and not ordered the Fairmiles to pick up survivors." Mitchell lowered his eyes.

"A lot more men would have died. They picked up all the survivors of the two ships."

"Yes, but maybe not mine." Mitchell looked up at Ryan, "Isn't that a terrible thing to say?"

Ryan shrugged. "What about the Commodore, what did he say?"

"Oh, he said I did the best I could. Linda was relieved."

"I told her that," said Ryan with some satisfaction.

"You did?"

"Yeah, the morning I saw you. She asked to speak to me after I was finished with you. I told her you'd done everything by the book and not to worry."

Mitchell looked at Ryan for a moment, then quietly said, "Thank you."

A little embarrassed, Ryan changed the topic. "Look, Mitch, did Linda tell you why I was coming over?"

"Yes, she said you had something to bounce off me," replied Mitchell, motioning for Ryan to take a seat.

"Right," said Ryan, sitting down. "Let me start at the beginning. First, we have a U-boat leaving France minus most of her torpedoes but with a squad of commandos on board."

Mitchell said, "Raiding party?"

"That's what you'd think. Except they head across the Atlantic and land at the top of Labrador."

"Labrador? Are you sure they landed?"

"Fairly. But wait, it gets better. There's nothing up there but a *Canadian Weather Service* automated weather station."

"Then they were after that," interrupted Mitchell.

"Wrong again. They didn't touch it, and there's no such thing as the *Canadian Weather Service.*"

"So, they landed it."

"Probably. But why the commandos? There's nobody up there. And why the direct trip? That's the sort of thing you do as part of a patrol."

"Where is he now, do you know?"

"Yes," answered Ryan. "He was D/F'd east of Cape Bonavista a few hours ago."

"Maybe he's looking for targets, planning to go into Conception Bay. Hoping to make it three strikes," Mitchell answered bitterly, thinking of the previous two attacks.

"There's nothing there, Mitch. Commodore Taylor halted all use of the Wabana anchorage until nets are in place."

"The U-boat's skipper doesn't know that."

"But yes he does, Mitch."

At Mitchell's surprised look, Ryan continued. "I shouldn't tell you this, but...we think there is a spy. Either on Bell Island or on one of the ore carriers themselves, although we're running out of suspect ships. The two that were there both times, *Fort Rose* and

PBM27, were sunk. So, that leaves a spy on Bell Island itself, although that seems unlikely. Small community like that, even counting all the miners, everyone knows everyone else. Nevertheless, the U-boat would know there's nothing to attack. Unless they want to sink a couple of fishing boats, and that isn't worth the risk."

"So, where is he going?" asked Mitchell.

"I don't know. We've picked up a lot of U-boat transmissions off St. John's and south. They're popping up all over the place. And the Americans sank a sub this afternoon off Cape Race."

"Maybe they're setting up a patrol line?"

"Possibly, but the major convoy routes are northeast of St. John's, not south. Why assemble a wolfpack to attack local convoys when the main routes are east...or off Halifax?"

Mitchell and Ryan discussed the problem for the next hour or so until they heard the front door open and Dr. Halley walk in. Mrs. O'Brien took his hat and coat. Both men stood when the Doctor entered the living room and Mitchell introduced Lieutenant Ryan.

"Business or pleasure, Lieutenant?" asked the Dr. Halley.

"Lieutenant Ryan was running something past me, sir," volunteered Mitchell.

"Don't tire him out, Lieutenant. He's still not one hundred percent," advised the Doctor. Changing the subject, he asked Ryan, "You're not going to the big dance at the *Knights of Columbus* tonight, Lieutenant?"

"Call me Frank, sir. And no, I'm on duty at 2300. A couple of beers and I'd be asleep at my desk by midnight."

"Too bad," said Dr. Halley. "Sounds like quite a time. I was listening to it on the radio as I drove home. *Uncle Tim's Barn Dance* is playing and apparently the place is blocked."

"Yes, sir," said Ryan.

"Well, I'll leave you to it. Mrs. O'Brien has supper for me in the dining room. Nice meeting you, Frank." At Ryan's "my pleasure", he grabbed his pipe off the mantle and departed. Mitchell and Ryan sat back down.

Ryan said, "Boy, the escort crews and flyboys are going to be miffed in the morning."

"Why?" asked Mitchell.

"I dropped by Operations on the way here. All available escorts and planes have been sent out on night patrol. Something's brewing and the Boss sent them off to find out what."

"Maybe that's it," said Mitchell slowly.

"What's it?"

"Maybe that's the plan. Draw off all our forces and then attack St. John's."

"Wouldn't work."

"Why not?"

"Because all the gun emplacements, both overlooking the Narrows and in town, are still manned. He'd be blown out of the water. That's if he could get in. There's still the anti-torpedo baffles and the anti- submarine net across The Narrows. No, that's not it."

"Well, how about somewhere else?" said Mitchell. Then added, "Perhaps the air field? With all the planes out, they'd be somewhat undermanned."

"That's a thought! How far is it from the coast?" said Ryan, looking about the room. "We need a map!" They went over to the large antique globe in the corner and spun it around. Finding the spot, Ryan said, "Maybe two or three miles. But there'd still be too many men there."

"Even with the dance on?"

"Yes. With all the patrols out, there'd be the ground crews, firefighters, air traffic controllers...medical people, sentries."

"They'd need to draw them off."

"A diversion. But what?"

"I don't know," said Mitchell. Both men looked at each other, stymied.

OFFSHORE, *U573* QUIETLY BROKE THE SURFACE, water cascading out of the drain holes along the Conning Tower and casing. She nosed her way into Middle Cove and halted approximately 200 metres from the rocky beach. Once more, shadows appeared on the forward casing but this time, unencumbered by heavy equipment or the civilians, the rubber rafts were quickly launched and the commando squad struck out for shore. They landed without mishap. Two sentries again took station at appropriate protective positions, ready to initiate a withering enfilade if they were discovered. No alarm was raised and the boats were secreted under cut boughs at the tree line. The team formed up into two lines, with *Hauptmann* Heydemann and *Unteroffizier* Knorr, Heydemann's XO, at the front of each. With parade ground precision, the troop double-timed it up the dirt road from the landing site.

Still on electric motors, *U573* headed out of the small cove. When she reached sufficient depth, the U-boat silently submerged. Now the waiting began in earnest.

THE *KNIGHTS OF COLUMBUS* HOSTEL on Harvey Road was filled to capacity. A cross-section of the Armed Forces was present; RCN sailors and officers from the escorts alongside, RCAF personnel, merchant seamen, Newfoundland Regiment, Canadian Army, Americans from Fort *Pepperrell,* plus local women and those of the women's forces. Biddy O'Toole was belting out "Don't Sit Under the Apple Tree (with anyone else but me)" by the King Sisters.

Nobody paid any attention to the man in the bulky overcoat as he moved down the hall and disappeared into the back stairwell. He climbed the stairs, two at a time, until he reached the top landing. There, nailed to the wall, he found the ladder leading to the attic above the Main Hall. He went up the ladder and through the access hatch, and crawled along the ceiling until he was over the dance floor.

He took a *Coca-Cola* bottle of petrol from his coat, uncorked it and splashed its contents around the fibreboard underside of the ceiling. That done, he took another out of his pocket. It was the same as the first but had a rag wick hanging out of the neck. He lit it and placed the bottle upright in the centre of the gasoline-soaked area. He crawled back to the hatch and slid down the ladder.

A minute later, he exited from the front entrance, his wide-brimmed hat shading his face. He bumped into a couple entering the Hall and, in accented English, said, "Excuse me." Then he disappeared into the night.

The *Coke* bottle burned like a candle for a while before finally exploding, unheard by those below over the music of the orchestra. The gas-soaked ceiling quickly caught and, in no time, the entire attic area was an inferno. For five minutes no one below suspected the danger above.

Until the ceiling collapsed! Flaming debris ignited paper tablecloths, curtains, and people's clothes. The crowd headed to the side doors - locked for security reasons. The fire exits were clearly marked, but they opened inward and, against the press of the mob, could offer no escape. Blind panic ensued.

Outside, the flames licking from windows and the screams of those trapped inside quickly brought the local firefighters. The magnitude of the blaze was beyond their capabilities and a call went out for assistance.

It was received at Fort *Pepperell*, the American army base overlooking Quidi Vidi Lake, Camp *Lester* on Blackmarsh Road, the RCN barracks at Buckmasters' Field, and at RCAF Air Station *Torbay* outside St. John's. Medical personnel, firefighters, and any able-bodied men were desperately needed to combat a fire that could, quite easily, destroy the entire city of old, woodframe, tinder-dry buildings.

HAUPTMANN HEYDEMANN RAISED HIS ARM to halt the troop. They'd reached what his map indicated to be Torbay Road, about two kilometres north of the air base. The thin beams of blacked-out headlights were approaching from the same direction. As they neared, Heydemann could make out the distinctive shape of a military jeep. Pulling over across from the commandos, two soldiers in spotless white helmets, gunbelts and leggings jumped out.

"*Feldgendarmerie*!" hissed Knorr, thumbing the safety on his *Schmeisser MP-40* submachine gun.

One of the Military Police strode over towards them. The driver stayed by the jeep, hand on his sidearm. Heydemann met the MP halfway. The man started to salute, glancing at *Heydemann's* collar and sleeve for some indication of rank, then said, "Sir?"

Knowing the question, the *Hauptmann* answered, "Captain Carl Hydeman, US Marine Corps. We're a special unit, Sergeant. We don't wear insignia. Weren't you told we were out here training?" Heydemann used the

Anglicized version of his name and rank, and effected a slight twang to his normally private-school English.

"No, sir," replied the sergeant. "As a matter of fact, we were dispatched to check on a U-boat sighting."

"A U-boat? That's hardly likely, is it, Sergeant?"

"No, sir. But ever since those ships were torpedoed off Bell Island, we get one or two reports a day. We have to check each one out."

"Yes. I understand, Sergeant" said the German, not knowing what the man was talking about.

"You haven't seen anything, have you, sir?"

"Like a squad of Kraut troops off a U-boat, Sergeant?" Heydemann smiled, trying to look convincing.

"No, sir, of course not." The sergeant eyed the officer in front of him. "Sir, would you have *any* ID?"

"No, I wouldn't, I'm afraid" Heydemann said, suspecting his bluff was being called. "Look, son. Like I said, we're Special Ops. We don't wear insignia or carry ID. Our fatigues are the only thing to prevent us from being shot as spies if captured on an operation! Although, I understand that *Herr* Hitler's has ordered all captured commandos shot on sight as spies." He was telling the truth.

"I'm sorry, sir," said the MP, not quite convinced. "I'm going to have to check this out with Headquarters."

The sergeant turned and headed back to the jeep to use the radio. Heydemann quietly unclipped his holster and heard Knorr, behind him, gently slide the bolt back on his machinegun. Heydemann slowly drew his Lüger and thumbed the safety, all the while keeping his eyes on the MP's retreating back.

Suddenly, a voice blared from the radio. The driver leaned in and grabbed the microphone. He spoke into it, listened to the reply, then shouted to the other man, "Jack, forget it. They want us back at HQ. Pronto! There's a big fire in town."

The sergeant turned back to Heydemann, who concealed his pistol behind his thigh. "Sorry to have bothered you, sir. I'm afraid I'll have to file a report on this, so you'll probably get a call in the morning." He saluted.

"No problem, Sergeant," said Heydemann, returning the salute. "I'll tell them how diligent you were."

"Thank you, sir." The sergeant trotted back to the jeep and climbed in. He waved as the driver turned the vehicle in the middle of the road and headed back the way they'd come, spitting gravel. Heydemann holstered his pistol and returned to his men. He winked at Knorr, who slid the bolt back on his weapon.

CHAPTER TWENTY-SEVEN

THE GRANDFATHER CLOCK IN THE HALL chimed the bottom of the hour. Frank Ryan stood up, suddenly realizing the time. He and Mitchell had been talking for almost three and a half hours and Ryan was due at Headquarters. The phone rang and Mrs. O'Brien answered it.

While Ryan and Mitchell exchanged pleasantries, Dr. Halley took the call. He finished and walked into the living room, his face the colour of chalk. Mitchell and Ryan both stared at him. In disbelief, he said, "The *K of C* is on fire. There are people trapped inside."

Ryan and Mitchell met each other's eyes. Mitchell said, "That's it!"

Dr. Halley, not comprehending, looked at the two men and said quietly, "They need me at St. Claire's. Victims are starting to come in." He went out of the room, met the housekeeper, who had his coat and medical bag in her hand, and rushed out of the house.

Mitchell and Ryan heard the sound of the Doctor's car starting, followed by the screech of tires as it tore out of the driveway.

"What do we do?" asked Mitchell.

"I don't know," replied Ryan.

"Call Operations?"

"And tell them what? There're German commandos - off a U-boat - going to attack the air base? They wouldn't believe it. Hell, I wouldn't believe it!"

"Well, we should at least call the Base and tell them something might be up. To double the sentries or something," pleaded Mitchell.

"You're right," said Ryan, trying to calm the young Lieutenant. He picked up the phone and dialled. "No answer. The fire must have cut off the main telephone lines through town. Now what?"

"We have to go out there."

"And do what?"

"Tell them...warn them to be ready...SOMETHING!" said Mitchell with growing desperation.

"Okay," said Ryan, mind reeling. "Come on, grab your coat, my car's outside."

Mrs. O'Brien was already at the door with their hats and coats. They grabbed them with a quick *Thank you*, and rushed outside to Ryan's grey staff car, Mitchell's left arm holding his ribs. Ryan, in the driver's seat, pushed the starter as Mitchell shut his door, grunting as he did so.

Ryan looked at him, and asked, "You okay to do this?"

Through clenched teeth, Mitchell hissed, "Go!"

Ryan put the car in gear and peeled off down the driveway. Without slowing, they careened out onto Topsail Road, then headed east on Water Street. With the City observing blackout regulations, they could easily see the glow of the blaze, despite being a mile away.

They drove in silence, occasionally pulling to the curb to let emergency vehicles pass. They went up Hill O'Chips, past the anti-aircraft gun emplacement, and turned onto Duckworth Street, making a left at the Naval Headquarters to King's Bridge Road. They sped down the hill, sparks flying as the bottom of the car hit the pavement at the road's intersection with The Boulevard. They tore up Kenna's Hill, finally turning onto the newly-paved Torbay Road at the top. Now it was a straight run out to the air base.

THE SMOKE FORMED AN IMPENETRABLE BARRIER a foot above his head as Sub-Lieutenant James Martin crawled along the floor looking for a way out of the *Knights of Columbus*. The acrid fumes burned his throat, despite the handkerchief he held against his mouth, and his eyes watered continuously.

Someone stumbled over him in the gloom and fell, pinning him to the floor. He could barely make out the face but could see the whites of the man's eyes, wide with panic. He had never seen such absolute, blind terror before in his life. The man got up and ran back the way he'd come.

Martin heard screams and pounding to his right, and tried to get his bearings. That must be the Hall, he thought, fighting to remember the floor plan. The washrooms were to the right of that and the main entrance down the corridor between the two. If he just kept going in this direction, he should be able to get out.

It had all happened so fast! He'd been in the washroom, splashing cold water on his face to cool himself, when the single light bulb dimmed and went out. He heard screams and someone yell, "Fire!" He opened the door and was met by a billow of hot, black smoke. He dropped to all fours to get under the cloud and started to crawl along the smooth linoleum, looking for an escape route. He'd gotten about twenty feet when the man had stumbled over him.

He continued straight, following the pattern on the floor to keep from getting lost. His breathing was getting more laboured and he felt dizzy. Don't pass out, he told himself, just a little bit further. But he was losing the battle. He started to cough and sharp pains racked his chest; it felt like his lungs were burning. Suddenly, he threw up and collapsed, face-down into the mess. This is it, he thought. I've had it.

Someone kicked him in the ribs. He felt a hand grab his shirt at the shoulder and start to drag him forward on the floor. Barely conscious and unable to struggle, he allowed himself to be pulled along. He could hear the man's grunts and coughs but could do nothing. Well, at least they were going in the right direction, he thought.

He felt fresh air on his face, opened his eyes, and could see stars. He was picked up bodily, like a child, and carried for a distance. He heard shouts and saw flashing lights. His rescuer laid him down and wiped his eyes with a wet cloth.

"You'll be all right now, son."

He knew that voice!

He gripped the arm that held him and struggled to focus properly. The face above him became clear and despite the scorched hair, missing eyebrows and the soot, Martin knew who it was.

"Thanks, Chief," he croaked.

Chief Petty Officer RJ Vaughan of HMCS *Dartmouth* just smiled, then coughed and spat into his handkerchief. Bloody junior officers, he thought.

PRIVATE STAN KORNESKI of Dauphin, Manitoba, sat in the guardhouse wondering what the heck was going on. He'd been sitting, enjoying the music from the big dance at the *Knights of Columbus* on his radio and cursing his bad luck for drawing guard duty. Suddenly, the broadcast stopped. Then, a half hour ago, the whole base emptied as fire engines, ambulances, and truckloads of men whizzed past the small shack, heading for town.

Korneski glanced out the window, then looked again. A squad of soldiers were marching towards him down the centre of the roadway. Leaving his shack as they approached, the sentry was grabbed from behind and his throat opened with the sharp blade of *Unteroffizier* Knorr's double-sided blade. Korneski died quickly as he bled out and slumped into the German commando's arms. Knorr dragged Korneski's body into the guardhouse and Liebe, the only other English-speaking member of the team aside from Heydemann, took his place. The rest of the commandos trotted in through the gate and headed towards the aircraft hangars.

Once there, they fanned out in two-man teams over the airfield, leaving the odd-man out to act as sentry. They planted small incendiary devices wherever a suitable hiding place presented itself - on fuel trucks or parked aircraft, on ammunition lockers, oil drums - anywhere that would cause the most fire and damage.

After planting a charge on a nearby fuel truck, Heydemann and his partner entered a hangar. They heard voices and Heydemann indicated by hand signals to stop. He crouched down and peeked in through a doorway. It was the ground crew in the lounge, waiting for the patrol planes to return, their backs to the door. Too many to take on, Heydemann scooted across the doorway and gestured for the other man to follow. He did, silently imitating the Captain's actions.

They found a darkened spot at the rear of the building by some 50-gallon drums. Heydemann reached into a pouch on his belt and took out a charge. Signalling to his accomplice, he was passed the detonator. He set the timer and attached the explosive to one of the drums. After confirming the timer was running, the two headed out the way they had come in, again skirting the open doorway to the lounge.

Outside they met the rest of the commandos, who had regrouped in the lee of an outbuilding. Heydemann checked the luminescent dial on his watch – twenty-five minutes. That's all it had taken, and they were well ahead of schedule as it was. They formed up and again double-timed it to the front gate - hiding in plain sight. They arrived just as headlights approached.

DOCTOR WILLIAM HALLEY SURVEYED THE SCENE before him. Every available space was occupied, including the floor of the waiting room, at St. Clare's Mercy Hospital. Doctors, nurses, medical corpsmen from Camp *Lester*, plus sickberth attendants from HMCS *Avalon,* and hospital corpsmen from Fort *Pepperrell,* went from stretcher to stretcher. So did Father Connolly, the hospital chaplain, reciting *Prayers for the Dead* over those who were beyond help.

Most of the injuries were burns or smoke inhalation. The odd one had broken bones from leaping to safety from an open window. The smell of smoke pervaded the entire area and many of the victims cried out in pain, or just moaned. Those in Father Connolly's care were silent.

"Doctor Halley!"

One of the nursing sisters called from the side of a new arrival, a young woman about the same age as his daughter. Thank God Linda was on duty tonight, he thought. He knew she wouldn't be one of the casualties. How many fathers were now trying to find out if their daughters were safe.

He walked over to the young woman. Just a girl, really. Her hair was gone and her dress burnt onto her skin. Her arm was charred and she didn't appear to be breathing. Doctor Halley lifted her wrist and checked for a pulse. There wasn't one. He put his stethoscope to the girl's chest, listened for a moment, then removed the earpieces.

"Nothing we can do, Sister," he said and covered the girl with a sheet. Another one for Father, he thought, and headed for the next arrival.

RYAN GEARED DOWN as they neared the guardhouse, and the sentry stepped out. He was dressed in black and grey camouflage fatigues and, as he leaned into the passenger window, smelled faintly of diesel fumes. Must be all the *Deuce and a Half*s going in and out of the base, though Ryan, absently. He and Mitchell both showed the young soldier their IDs. Ryan asked if everything was all right. "Nothing unusual?" he inquired.

"No, sir. Quiet as a graveyard," answered the soldier and waved them on. As Ryan put the car back in gear, he noticed a squad of men to his left. They were also in cammo-fatigues and, while standing easy, their weapons were at the ready. Ryan accelerated and they drove through the silent base.

Suddenly, he slammed on the brakes, almost sending Mitchell into the windshield.

"W-what!" exclaimed Mitchell.

"That sentry...those soldiers. Didn't they look odd to you?"

"Why?"

"Both were wearing black and grey camouflages, ours are green. They had no insignia that I could see, rank or regiment. And those guns weren't any I've seen before. You?"

"Maybe they're Special Forc...," said Mitchell, then realized. "The Jerry Commandos!" he exclaimed.

"Yeah," said Ryan, his suspicions confirmed. He put the car into a U-turn and headed back to the gate, pedal to the metal.

"You're not going back? We're not even armed!" said Mitchell, incredulous.

Ryan reached under his seat, pulled out a Colt .45 and chambered a round, steering with his knee. "There's one under your seat too," he told Mitchell.

"This is suicide," said Mitchell, rummaging around under his seat with his hand. He found the gun just as they reached the guardhouse. The sentry and the others were gone. Ryan got out of the car, gun in hand, safety off. He looked in the shack and, upon seeing Private Korneski, quickly turned his head and spewed the contents of his stomach on the asphalt. Only then noticing the bloody pavement.

Mitchell was now out of the car, his alarm evident. He looked at Ryan's expression and, knowing the answer, asked anyway. "The sentry?"

Ryan nodded his head while wiping his mouth with his sleeve and got back into the sedan. Mitchell followed. Ryan put it in reverse, straightened, and roared through the base until he came to the hangars.

"They must have already planted the explosives," he said, getting out of the car. The two men ran to the nearest hangar, Mitchell in obvious discomfort. They found the ground crew in the lounge, just as Heydemann had. Ryan burst in, gun in one hand, ID in the other.

"I'm Lieutenant Ryan, Naval Intelligence" he shouted at the startled men. "We think there're bombs planted here and around the airfield." They didn't move, staring at Ryan, open-mouthed. "Come on, before we're all blown to pieces!" Ryan shouted.

That did it. Someone hit the alarm; a siren screamed and revolving red lights added to the urgency. So much for blackout regulations, thought Mitchell. The ground crew grabbed battle lanterns and spread out across the airfield, Ryan yelling out to them to alert the other hangars and the tower. One by one, alarms went off all over the airfield. The night erupted into chaos.

Ryan and Mitchell surveyed the hangar they were in through the dull glow of the work-lights overhead. "What are we looking for?" Mitchell asked, scanning uncertainly. There were just so many places!

"How should I know? I'm just a newspaperman!" Ryan retorted. He thought for a second, then said aloud,

"They couldn't hope to blow the place up, too big and it would take a lot of heavy charges..."

"But they could burn it down," suggested Mitchell, scanning the cavernous space for flammable materials or equipment. Looking at the various housed aircraft under repair, he ventured, "How about these patrol planes. Blow one up, they all go?"

"Sure," answered Ryan. "Attach an incendiary to a gas tank or..." he saw the 50-gallon drums with *AVGAS* stencilled on the sides. "Those!" he said, pointing to the oil drums in the opposite corner. "There's enough aviation fuel in them to burn down the whole damn airfield!" The two men ran over, branching off as they reached them to cover more ground.

"Nope!...nope!...nope!...nope!" shouted Ryan in frustration as he went from barrel to barrel, knowing instinctively that time was getting short.

Suddenly Mitchell yelled, "Found it!"

Ryan rushed over to where Mitchell squatted by a barrel. The two men looked at each other. The explosive resembled an oversized sardine can with a small clock attached. Two wires led from the timer to the charge.

"Now what?" asked Mitchell.

"Pull out the wires," answered Ryan.

"What if that sets it off?"

"Maybe we should just cut one of the wires?" replied his companion.

"You got a knife?" Mitchell asked.

"Nope. You?"

"No. Goddamn it, what are we supposed to do?" yelled Mitchell, his panic growing.

Looking at the timer ticking towards zero, Ryan said, "Another thirty seconds and it won't make any difference." He reached over, his hand going back and forth from one wire to the other, a noticeable tremor showing. "Screw it!" he mumbled under his breath, and pulled both wires off at the same time. The timer ticked down towards zero

Ryan and Mitchell held their breaths. The clock stopped. Time stood still. Suddenly, they heard a dull PPUUFF outside and, through the open hangar doors, saw a fuel truck erupt into flames.

"That's one," said Mitchell. Again they waited but there were no more explosions. Men started to return to the hangar as Ryan and Mitchell walked out. One man came forward and said, "Looks like we got all but that one, sir."

"No kidding!" said Ryan, his face illuminated by the burning truck 30 yards away, now surrounded by men playing foam onto the flames. He started to laugh. One by one, the rest joined in, howling and slapping each other's backs in relief. Shortly, a jeep screeched to a halt in front of them and an officer jumped out. He wore the insignia of a full bird Colonel.

"What the HELL is going on here?!" he demanded.

"Sir, you wouldn't believe me if I told you," said Ryan, and tossed him the disarmed explosive.

OFFSHORE, *U573* lay stopped, trimmed down with her decks awash. On the bridge, *Hauptmann* Heydemann and *Kapitän-Leutnant* Schilling peered landward over the coaming. Binoculars to their eyes, they strained to see the conflagration confirming success of the raid.

The commandos' return trip had been swift and uneventful. They'd made a clean getaway. Arriving on the beach ahead of schedule, they signalled the U-boat with a shaded blue light and, receiving a reply, uncovered the rubber boats. They'd rowed to the submarine, sank the rafts, and were now awaiting the fruits of their labour.

"Any second now," mumbled Heydemann.

They could hear distant alarms and a red hue engulfed the western horizon. After a short time there was a small flash, then nothing. Schilling lowered his binoculars and looked at his companion. "That's it? I thought there'd be more to it."

"There should be," said Heydemann, bitter disappointment in his voice.

They waited but nothing else happened. The *Hauptmann* turned and vanished below. Schilling stayed up, hoping they were wrong and, any second, the sky would light up with explosions and flames. But no. It was not to be.

At his order, the lookouts dropped down the hatch, Schilling following behind. The vents along the saddle tanks opened, spewing vapour, and the U-boat sank from view.

CHAPTER TWENTY-EIGHT

THE SKY WAS CLEAR and full of stars. It was cold but the first snow of the winter had yet to fall. HMCS *Ancaster* rode the gentle swells at a steady 8 knots, making the windchill factor on the exposed bridge close to freezing. The men of the watch were bundled up in heavy duffle coats and fur-lined sea boots but occasionally someone stamped their feet or rubbed their arms to maintain circulation. The silence was further interrupted with quiet orders or occasional reports, and the sound of the sea as it sluiced along the sides of the ship.

Lieutenant Mike Duffy, RCNVR, *Ancaster*'s First Lieutenant, or *Jimmy the One* to the lower deck, sipped his mug of cocoa and cursed his bad luck.

He'd been all lined up with Patsy Aylward tonight. No mean feat, considering her reputation and the number of

lonely young officers aware of that reputation. He'd been looking forward to a few drinks and a scuff or two at the *Knights of Columbus* this evening, and afterwards, well, who knew what might happen afterwards.

Just as he thought his night was set, the Flag Officer, Newfoundland Force, ordered all available escorts out on patrol. Something was brewing, Captain (D) said, and Commodore Taylor wanted to know what. *Ancaster* was detailed to cover the approaches

to St. John's Harbour from Cape Spear as far north as Quidi Vidi Gut. They'd gotten underway at suppertime and plodded back and forth across the Narrows for the next few hours, asdic pinging and radar probing. Nothing was detected.

However, just as things settled down into a humdrum routine, they got the call from Operations to head

for Middle Cove. A U-boat had been
sighted offshore.

Yeah, right, thought the Lieutenant.
And pigs fly! Ever since the attacks at
Bell Island, and the sinking of the
Sydney to Port-aux-Basque passenger
ferry *Caribou* in the Fall, the locals
were seeing damned U-boats in every
wave. One had even been reported
flying through the air! FONF was
reported to have said that if the Nazis
had as many U-boats as the locals
reported, he could walk from St.
John's to Liverpool without getting his
feet wet! But at least HMCS
Ancaster's current assignment was
better than going back and forth
across the Harbour Approaches like
some clockwork mouse!

Duffy lit a cigarette and sauntered
over to the narrow, curtain-covered
entrance to the asdic hutch at the
front of the bridge. Having recently
completed her work-up after a refit at
Charleston, South Carolina, HMCS
Ancaster was a little more up-to-date
than many of her sisters. She had an
enlarged bridge, sporting a 20mm

Oerlikon on each wing, the new Type 271 radar, and an improved asdic in a separate compartment just forward of the steering position. You still had to poke your head in to check on progress but at least it was better than stomping on the deck or hooting into a voicepipe to the compartment below, as had been the case in HMCS *York*, his previous appointment.

Duffy pulled back the curtain and entered the tiny room. Bartlett and Coombs sat hunched over their equipment, Coombs' head encased in large rubber earphones. Sub-Lieutenant Paul Boundridge, RCNVR, *Ancaster*'s anti-submarine officer, stood behind the two men, a hand resting on each man's shoulder.

"Anything?" Duffy asked, for what seemed like the hundredth time.

"No, sir," replied Boundridge, as if it *had* been the hundredth time.

"Carry on."

Boundridge mumbled something under his breath about rather going to the pub, which Duffy ignored. He couldn't blame the crew. He was just as pissed at their last minute duty. Duffy turned and stepped through the curtain back up onto the bridge. He surreptitiously checked the compass heading as he walked over to the large wooden chair bolted to the deck at the rear. As Officer of the Watch, it was his responsibility to ensure that they were on course. But, he didn't want the young sailor at the wheel to think he was checking up on him. Duffy believed in giving his men confidence in their abilities by actions, not just lip service.

He sat down and took a mouthful of cocoa from the mug in his hand. He liked nights like this actually, and if it weren't for his spoiled plans, this evening's duty might almost be enjoyable. Duffy looked at his watch. 0055. He was supposed to call the Skipper at 0100, another 5 minutes. Then Duffy could go below and get a few hours' sleep. Alone, he thought regretfully.

"Sir, contact bearing 290!" Sub-Lieutenant Boundridge appeared in the doorway of the asdic hut, excitement clearly showing on his face.

"What's the range, Sub?"

"About 2,000 yards, sir."

"Maher," yelled Duffy, remembering the young seaman's name, "steer 290."

"290, aye, sir," replied the teenager at the wheel, frankly surprised that *Jimmy* knew his name. He didn't like referring to the Lieutenant as that but the rest of the men did and young Charlie Maher wanted, more than anything, to fit in.

Duffy plucked the handset from the bulkhead next to him and called the Skipper. So much for my couple of hours sleep, he thought, as he heard the familiar voice answer the phone.

ANCASTER'S ASDIC SIGNAL sounded like pebbles being thrown against the hull of the U-boat. *Kapitän-Leutnant* Schilling looked up from his writing. *U573* was at 20 metres, heading east, submerged after leaving Middle Cove. He hadn't planned to surface and make the run out to sea until they were at least five miles from the coast. Schilling was in his cabin writing out his report of the raid on the air base. Not much to write, really, other than it was a dismal failure. At least they hadn't lost anyone or been detected. Yet!

The pebbles were thrown again, and Schilling got up and headed for the Control Room. First Watch Officer von Blücher was just asking *Zentralemaat* Reith to get the *Kaleu* when Schilling popped through the hatchway.

"I was just calling you..." started von Blücher.

"Report, Number One," snapped his captain.

"Sir, we've got a destroyer off the port bow. It appears to have detected us and is closing to investigate," replied von Blücher.

"What's the depth?"

"Fifty metres, sir."

"*Scheisse!*" swore Schilling. Not enough sea room to evade. "How far to deep water?"

"Two thousand metres, *Kaleu*," answered the *Erster Wache Offizier*.

So, we have to get past the destroyer first, thought Schilling. "Okay, here's what we do. We'll go to 40 metres and head straight for the destroyer. That will give him less of a target and the wash of his own screws will mask our asdic return. We'll still get a drubbing but, once we're past him, we'll be in deep water." Schilling turned and ordered to the Control Room at large, "Silence throughout the boat! Rig for depth charge attack!"

As the orders were passed down the line, all water tight hatches were dogged shut, except the forward Control Room hatch. Through that one, *Kapitän-Leutnant* Schilling would get reports from *Funkmaat* Petersen on the hydrophones. All hands could hear *Ancaster* charge in. Petersen yelled, "Depth charges dropped!" and they held on. This was going to be rough.

The depth charges were set for seventy-five feet and, while badly shaking the U-boat, did little damage. *Ancaster* roared past them and looped to port. Schilling maintained course and Petersen reported that the corvette had overtaken them and was passing across their path directly ahead, cutting them off. Another barrage detonated forward of the U-boat, this time set at one hundred feet. The submarine staggered as the blastwaves hit.

Schilling walked over to the chart table to port; von Blücher followed. He lifted the peak of his crumpled officers' hat to see better in the dim overhead light, and studied the chart. Looking at von Blücher over his shoulder, he said, "He's not going to let us out."

"No, sir," replied the young First Officer.

"Well, if we can't get out, then we'll go further inshore and bottom. I understand their asdic doesn't work very well in really shallow water. *Leutnant*, fire a *Bold* and take us as close to shore as you can. Put us down at twenty metres."

"Aye, aye, *Kaleu*," replied von Blücher.

The *Bold* was an asdic decoy, sort of like an underwater smokescreen. To

the British it was known as an SBT-
Submarine Bubble Target. The device
created a mass of bubbles underwater
intended to simulate the echo return
of a U-boat. Depending on the depth,
the effect lasted upwards of 25
minutes.

The U-boat made a tight arc to
starboard. A small canister was
ejected from the Pill-thrower, a
miniature torpedo tube located in the
aft *torpedoraum*. Behind the resulting
disturbance, *U573* put her stern to the
warship, trying to present the
smallest asdic target possible. They
headed in to the coast. Occasionally,
von Blücher ordered a reading from
the depth sounder and tried to confirm
their position on the chart.

The manoeuvre took twenty
minutes. Finally, von Blücher
announced, "*Kaleu*, this is about as far
as we can go. Depth is twenty metres."

"Very good, *Leutnant*. Put her on
the bottom." He turned towards the
open Control Room hatch forward and
asked, "Petersen, what's the destroyer
doing?"

"Sir, he's just going back and forth about fifteen hundred metres astern," replied the soundman. "He seems to have lost us. It's probably too shallow here to get a good return."

The U-boat settled onto the rocky bottom and heeled over slightly on its keel. The Captain ordered all hands not on duty to their bunks. Men who were not doing anything consumed less oxygen. But unfortunately they did more thinking and imaginations, especially amongst the younger crew, went wild. Schilling remained in the Control Room and waited patiently for something to happen.

He figured the destroyer had lost them in the shallow water but knew they were trapped. Re-enforcements were probably now on their way. Schilling didn't have much time. Even with all unnecessary machinery shut down and most of the crew in their bunks, the oxygen and batteries wouldn't last much longer than a day. And that was if he stayed put. He knew he didn't have a day. As soon as another warship turned up, they would start blanketing the area with depth charges. It would be only a matter of time before one found its mark and opened up the hull or blew the U-boat to the surface.

His options were limited; he could stay here, lying *doggo* on the bottom, and hope the destroyer went away. Probably not going to happen. Or, he could surface and try to fight his way out. Again, not much of an option. He was inshore, without much room to manoeuvre and, being broadside to the U-boat, the warship could bring all his guns to bear and start blasting away as soon as they surfaced.

The third alternative was to destroy all confidential documents, the codes and the *Schlüsselmaschine,* the ultra-secret coding machine, scuttle the boat and surrender. Most of the crew would survive the escape since they weren't very deep and all had been trained to use the *Tauchretter* escape gear. The only problem was that the enemy could salvage the U-boat and learn all her secrets. And for a dedicated naval officer like Schilling, that was unthinkable.

"*Kaleu*!" yelled Petersen from up forward, interrupting Schilling's contemplation, "fast screw noises bearing 070. Sounds like another destroyer."

Schilling looked at his watch in the gloom. They'd been bottomed one hour. That didn't take long, he thought. So now the ship above them had a friend. He'd been right. The captain of the destroyer was a smart man. He knew he didn't have enough charges to flush the U-boat out by himself. But with two of them, the outcome was a foregone conclusion. The only question now was, how long? And what was Schilling going to do about it?

Hauptmann Heydemann appeared in the hatchway, requesting permission to enter.

"Granted," snapped Schilling. Heydemann climbed through the hatch and walked towards the U-boat skipper, stepping over the odd seaman lying prone on the metal deck.

Heydemann faced Schilling and said in a low voice, "It appears our goose is cooked, Commander."

"It appears so, Captain," Schilling agreed.

"My men and I will not be taken alive," he said earnestly.

"Chances are, none of us will," answered Schilling, sardonically, pushing his oil-stained white officer's hat to the back of his head.

"Well, in that case, let's make it a good fight."

"I'm afraid it won't be much of a fight. More like a slaughter."

"It'd still be better than waiting down here like lambs, Commander. Wouldn't it?"

"Yes. I guess it would, Captain," replied Schilling thoughtfully. *Oberleutnant* von Blücher climbed through the aft Control Room hatch, having made a tour of the boat to reassure the crew.

"Number One!" called Schilling. Von Blücher closed the hatch, dogged it shut, then walked over. "We're going to Battle Surface. Prepare the forward tubes and assemble the gun crews. We'll surface bow on to the destroyers, fire all four tubes and man the guns.

Hopefully, our friends upstairs will scatter when they spot the torpedoes and we'll be able to blast our way out to open water."

"*Kaleu*, that's suicide. We'll be blown out of the water," said von Blücher quietly, eyes surveying the Control Room.

"We're dead men anyway, Lieutenant," injected Heydemann with a raised eyebrow. Von Blücher nodded resignedly.

"Then we're agreed," stated Schilling, looking at the two men. "Number One, make the preparations. Destroy all the secret documents and get the scuttling charge ready, just in case."

"Yes, sir."

"And tell the Chief we're going to need every knot he can get out of the engines," added Schilling. Von Blücher nodded again and headed once more for the aft Control Room hatch, rousing crewmen as he went.

Schilling turned to Heydemann. "You'd better get back to your troops. This is going to be *Haarstraubend.*"

"Hair-raising, Captain? This is just a day at the office for us!" chuckled the commando.

Schilling smiled. "When we surface, your men can go through the forward hatch again. But this time, warn them to stay low because the 105mm gun up forward will be firing and it's just abaft the hatch. I don't want one of them killed needlessly. Oh, and tell *Leutnant* Teschert to get the torpedoes ready for surface firing and then to report to me. Okay?"

"*Jawohl, Kaleu!*" smiled *Hauptmann* Heydemann, in adopted U-boat parlance, and snapped to attention. Schilling threw him a naval salute as the Captain turned and headed back through the open forward hatch. He's actually enjoying this, thought Schilling. Indeed, a rare breed.

The gun crews began assembling in the Control Room, 105mm and 75mm shells, and 50-cal machine guns cradled in their arms, and stood single file next to the ladder. Each was wearing a life vest and now familiar, coal-bucket shaped *Wehrmacht* helmet. They looked like a motley bunch but all were experienced seaman or petty officers, and knew what they had to do. *Leutnant zur See* Fritz Teschert, the Second Watch Officer, came through the forward Control Room hatch and approached the Captain.

"You know the plan?" Schilling asked him.

"Yes, *Kaleu*," answered the young officer. "The *Hauptmann* briefed me. All torpedoes are ready for surface firing. Safeties are off," meaning they would arm as soon as they left the tubes.

"Very good," replied his Captain.

Oberleutnant von Blücher climbed through the aft hatch. "All is ready, *Kaleu*," he reported. "The Chief will have the engines ready for Full Revolutions at your command. The after torpedo room is also ready, in case we get the opportunity to fire the stern tubes."

"Very good, Number One. Take us up on my order. Bring us around as we surface and send the gun crews up as soon as the hatch is clear. You go behind them and get to the UZO. Send down a bearing on the targets, but don't spend too much time. A rough one is good enough. If we hit one of them, great, but we'll only have seconds to get the eels off. So don't waste time polishing the cannonball, okay?" Schilling smiled. So did von Blücher at his captain's gallows humour.

Schilling surveyed the Control Room. All hands were at their stations, awaiting his orders. He wanted to know what the two warships were doing.

"Petersen!" he called out.

No answer.

He furrowed his brow and looked sharply at von Blücher.

"PETERSEN!"

Still no answer.

Schilling marched over to the forward hatchway and stopped, just as he was about to call the third time. He could see the soundman hunched over his receiver, eyes closed, a hand covering each of the earphones on his headset. He looked up slowly, sensing the *Kaleu*'s presence.

"Sir," he said, "I have a contact bearing 025. Sounds like a light engine. I'd say we have a small coaster heading our way. It's definitely not another destroyer."

"Well, I'll be damned!" exclaimed *Kapitän-Leutnant* Schilling, thoughtfully. "There might be a God, after all. If we live through this, I'll tell that to the *Fuehrer* personally." That got a few chuckles, as he knew it would. Turning around, he instructed the *Erster Wache Offizer*, "Number One, take us off the bottom, *slowly and quietly*. And get ready to give me Full Power on the electric motors."

"But...but, sir," stammered the confused First Officer. "What is it? What's heading towards us?"

"A chance, Number One. Just a chance," replied Schilling. And winked at the bewildered young man. The commandos might just be disappointed tonight.

THE OFFSHORE BREEZE filled the canvas sails, assisting the ten horse-power gasoline engine in its struggle to push the *Mary Sullivan* along at six knots. John Sullivan stood at the helm while his two brothers slept below. The schooner, which was named after their mother, was on her way from Pouch Cove to St. John's to pick up supplies for Mrs. Sullivan's general store. In her hold was salt fish, to be used as partial payment. They'd chosen to travel at night to avoid any U-boats that might be around. Schooners like the *Mary Sullivan* seldom got escorts.

John puffed on his pipe, which had once belonged to his late father, as had the *Mary Sullivan*. The eldest of the brothers, he was now the skipper; Mark, the next in line, was the mate; and Byron, barely sixteen, the deck hand.

He looked up at the stars to confirm he was on course. To starboard was the headland of Logy Bay and to port was the empty Atlantic. Or it should be empty. John saw the shadows of two ships. One detached and headed straight for him. At full speed, John judged from the size of the bow wave. He rapidly altered course to starboard, heading into Logy Bay as fast as the schooner could go. The warship was probably friendly, but he wasn't going to take any chances. If it was a Nazi raider, John wanted to be close to shore. The sudden change in direction sent the two brothers below to the deck, dumping them amongst a heap of boots, coats and blankets. They struggled out of the tangle and Mark scrambled up the stairs to the steering position at the stern.

"What the f...!" he started, but stopped abruptly as his older brother pointed to the fast-approaching corvette, off the port bow.

"We have company," John said, in the quiet, calm way that always infuriated Mark. Mark was a red-headed, quick-tempered man, a product of his mother's Irish heritage. John was more like their father. Young Byron appeared, just as the corvette intercepted them.

"This is His Majesty's Canadian Ship *Beauport*," blared the loud-hailer. "Please identify yourself and state your destination."

John cupped his hands around his mouth and yelled, "*Mary Sullivan* out o' Pouch Cove headin' fer Sin Jans."

"*Mary Sullivan*, come about and head east. We are conducting an anti-submarine sweep. Stay offshore til dawn."

"Dawn!" yelled Mark. "Go f..."

"Will do, *Beauport*," interrupted John. Mark started to argue but his older brother cut him off with that look, also like their father's, which brooked no discussion. He turned and went below to get dressed, as John put the schooner hard over and headed out to sea.

HMCS *Beauport* escorted them, about 200 yards ahead, until they were a couple of miles offshore, then departed at Full Speed. Shortly thereafter, the Sullivan brothers heard a massive depth charge attack.

"Get them sonsabitches!" yelled Mark.

The poor bastards, thought his older brother.

The *Mary Sullivan* continued east for the next few hours, until the first rays of the new day peeked over the horizon. The thunder of the depth charging had ceased an hour or so before. Whether the warships had sunk their sub or just given up the hunt, John didn't know. Although, he figured it was probably the former.

The sky got brighter and the wind picked up. The engine had sputtered to a halt hours ago, out of gas. It was time to come about and head for St. John's. He sent young Byron up the mast to see if he could spot a landmark astern. Mark came up on deck with a cup of tea. He passed it to John and was just about to speak when Byron exclaimed from above, "SWEET HOLY MOTHER OF GOD!"

Both men looked up. They could see their younger brother pointing to the water below. Mark ran over to the rail and looked down, expecting to see a shark or whale. He saw, instead, a dark bulk right underneath the *Mary Sullivan*, and at least twice as long. Air bubbles streamed from its sides. That's no whale, he thought. It's the effin' U-boat!

He turned and called to his brother, a tremor in his normally steady voice. "John. Don't argue, just bring 'er about. Now! And get us d'hell outta here!"

"Why...what is it?" started John.

"NOW!!" screamed his brother.

The obvious fear in Mark's face hastened John's hands as he spun the wheel hard-a-starboard. The boom whipped over his head and the sails luffed wildly until they once again caught the wind. Byron, who was all but forgotten above, held on for dear life as the schooner heeled over to her new course and the mast whipped about. Mark raced to the stern, expecting to see the U-boat surface in a welter of spray, and open fire. But nothing happened. He waited, stopping John's inquiry with a curt wave of his hand.

When it was obvious that the U-boat was not going to come up and blast them out of the water, he walked over to his older brother and explained. "It was d'U-boat, John. The effin' U-boat! Right underneat' us."

"What?!" replied his brother.

"Yes, b'y. Must've been un'er us since Logy Bay. Snuck away from dem warships, right un'er der noses."

"Well, I'll be goddamned," said John Sullivan, not without some reverence.

An hour's sailing brought them within sight of the Narrows, and they figured they were safe. John aimed the bow at the narrow opening, using Cabot Tower as his point of reference. His two brothers were both on deck, clad in sealskin parkas, as a light snow started to fall. God, what a night, he thought, and lit his pipe.

Mom will never believe us!

CHAPTER TWENTY-NINE

THE SNOW TURNED the ash to muck, further hindering the search for bodies. Men quietly sifted through the blackened remains of the *Knights of Columbus*, calling out only when something resembling a human being was discovered. So far this morning, they'd found ninety-nine.

The bodies were taken to the Catholic Cadet Corps Armoury next door, which was set up as a temporary morgue. Grieving parents and friends tried to identify a missing daughter, son, or comrade. Most could only guess, recognizing a bracelet or chain; or just a pair of shoes.

A QUARTER MILE AWAY, two officers presented themselves to the young Wren in the outer office of Flag Officer, Newfoundland Force. They'd been up all night preparing their report, and looked it. She noted the dark circles under their eyes and their unshaven faces. And would have offered them tea but figured they'd already had enough. She picked up the phone and announced their presence to her boss.

ALISTAIR MITCHELL AND FRANK RYAN sat quietly in front of Commodore C.R.H. Taylor's desk while he read their report. Finally, he finished, closed the folder, and laid it on the blotter in front of him.

"Quite an adventure, gentlemen," he concluded. Looking at Ryan, he asked, "Is this the only copy, Lieutenant?"

"No, sir. Mine is right here," replied Ryan, patting the case in his lap.

"May I have it, please?"

Ryan, surprised, slowly said, "Yes, sir, of course." He dug it out and passed it to Taylor who placed it on top of the one in front of him.

"Thank you, gentlemen, that is all."

Ryan and Mitchell looked at each other uncertainly. Ryan asked slowly, "Sir, my report?"

"Will stay with me, Lieutenant," said the Commodore.

"But, sir," protested Ryan, "I need to send it to NSHQ."

"No, you don't, Lieutenant. These reports will be buried in the deepest, darkest, most out of the way spot I can find!"

"What!" exclaimed Ryan and Mitchell, in unison.

"Why?" asked Mitchell. "It could happen again."

"That's just the point, Lieutenant Mitchell," replied Commodore Taylor, with a frown. "It could."

"But, but, sir...," started Ryan, flabbergasted at what he was hearing.

"Look, Lieutenant Ryan, Lieutenant Mitchell," said Taylor, softening, "The British and Americans both consider us a tolerance. Nothing more. They include us in their operational discussions more as a political courtesy than anything else. Oh, they want our men and ships, and everything, but they really don't think much of us. Well, maybe the Americans are a bit more sympathetic, considering their stellar performance along their own eastern seaboard last winter. But the bloody Brits... they're already blaming us for the losses in the Mid-Atlantic this past year. Poor training and leadership, they say. To hell with the fact that they escort the fast convoys and are at the top of the food chain when it comes to anti-submarine equipment. They need upgrading and training, they simple take it. Just leave it to the poor bloody Canadians to pick up the slack. Limey bastards!!!" Shaking his head, Taylor added, "Don't get me started!" The officer paused, looking defeated. "How long do you think it'd be before the Yanks took over here completely, if they found out about this? My God, they'd pee in their pants!

"Over the past three months, we've had a passenger ferry sunk off the west coast, lost four ships right in Conception Bay - no reflection on you, Lieutenant," he added, looking at Mitchell sympathetically. "We even sank one of our own bloody submarines off Trepassey!!! That's *Top Secret*, by the way.

"The fact is, gentlemen, if they ever found out that a U-boat successfully landed a weather station in Labrador, then launched a commando raid against one of our most important air bases..." Taylor paused. "...and almost got away with it! Why, they'd be in here so fast, it'd make your heads spin. No, gentlemen, this whole episode has to be buried...even from NSHQ.

Ryan and Mitchell were silent.

"One thing I do regret, though," continued Taylor, with real remorse in his voice, "is you two should each receive a medal. If it weren't for your quick thinking and, damnit, *bravery*, we'd already be kissing General Brandt's ass," referring to the habitually difficult American commander at St. John's.

Mitchell spoke up, "Sir, was the fire at the *K of C* arson?"

"Yes," replied Taylor. "No doubt. But, of course, there is no evidence as to whom. A couple of schoolboys discovered a Nazi radio in the hills over Kilbride a couple of weeks ago. They gave us a description of the suspect and the Constabulary have the place under surveillance, but so far, nobody's shown up."

"How many dead, sir?" asked Ryan.

"As far as we know, ninety-nine; seventy-three military and merchant marine, and twenty-six civilians. Whoever lit it knew what they was doing. It's a miracle there weren't more killed," said the Flag Officer, Newfoundland Force.

"So, you see, men, this can't get out. For all our sakes!" Then Taylor added, "However, I will put letters in both your service jackets. It will help with promotions in the future, although I know neither of you is regular navy. I'm afraid it's the best I can do." He held his hands out in a gesture of helplessness.

"Yes, sir," said Mitchell.

"Thank you, sir," said Ryan.

Both men stood, nodded to Commodore Taylor, and left the office. Taylor sighed resignedly. Those two deserve more, he thought. He picked up the two reports, stamped both TOP SECRET with red ink, and locked them in the bottom drawer of his desk.

Outside, Ryan and Mitchell looked at each other.

"Ours is not to reason why...," said Ryan, paraphrasing Tennyson.

"Well, you know what they say about the Navy," answered Mitchell, as they walked down the corridor.

"No, what?" asked Ryan.

"If you can't take a joke," replied Mitchell, "you shouldn't have joined."

EPILOGUE

ALISTAIR MITCHELL AND LINDA HALLEY married at the *Basilica of St. John the Baptist* overlooking downtown St. John's two months after Mitchell was discharged from hospital. He was promoted to Lieutenant-Commander shortly thereafter, and retook command of HMCS *Dartmouth* in Halifax. He left her to become Staff Officer (Operations) at St. John's a year later. Lieutenant Robert Blandford became First Officer and then Captain of *Dartmouth*, and got his U-boat in May 1944 when the corvette, the Royal Navy frigate *London,* and an RCAF Canso patrol plane sank *U722* in the mid-Atlantic. By then, *Lieutenant* James Martin was *Dartmouth*'s first officer, and was also decorated for that kill. Frank Ryan was promoted to Lieutenant-Commander and remained with Naval Intelligence at the Newfoundland Command for the rest of the war. He eventually married "the cute little Wren down the hall" and raised a family in St. John's. He died in 1994 at 74 years of heart failure.

U581 did not survive the war. She was sunk with all hands, 22 April 1945, by the American destroyers USS *Carter* and USS *Neal A. Scott* northwest of the Azores. Gerhard Tröjer was killed in action when *U166*, the U-boat he commanded, was sunk May 1944 by HMCS *Newcastle*. Konrad Wassermann survived the war and prospered in post-war West Germany but died on 2 November 1962, exactly twenty years after his attack at Bell Island.

Jean Carrier made it back to his homeland after the Normandy invasion. He found his wife and daughter safe in the south of France, having been sheltered during the war by Christian sympathisers.

A total of forty men lost their lives in the sinkings of the *Fort Rose* and *PBM27*. Several bodies washed ashore in the days and weeks following the attack and are buried on Bell Island. François Paquette's was not one of them.

Rogues Batiste was arrested by the *Gestapo* in 1944 in a round-up for the killing of two German sailors by the *Maquis*. He and 19 of his countrymen were shot in retaliation.

U573 and her crew made it safely back to Lorient, France, despite being the object of the RCN's first *Salmon* operation, codeword for "hunt to exhaustion." They enjoyed Christmas there; however, it was their last. The U-boat departed, still under the command of *Kapitän-Leutnant* Schilling, the following February for a lengthy operational tour in Southeast Asia. In November 1943, in the Java Sea off Indonesia, they came into the sights of the American submarine USS *Flounder* which sank the U-boat with all hands. She was discovered 60 miles (100km) northeast of

Karimunjawa Island in 2015 by divers from the *National Archaeology Centre*.

Hauptmann Karl Heydemann served with distinction for the remainder of the war and was awarded the *Knights Cross of the Iron Cross* at the Reich's Chancellery in Berlin by Adolph Hitler himself in 1943. He was killed on the steps of the Chancellery during the last days of the Battle for Berlin, May 1945. Heydemann has no known grave, although human remains were recently discovered in the area of central Berlin where the Chancellery once stood. They have yet to be identified.

Weather station *Kurt* continued to send weather reports across the Atlantic until its batteries ran out. It was not rediscovered, and identified as German, until July 1981. It is now on display at the *National War Museum* in Ottawa.

In 1993, a long-buried Flag Officer, Newfoundland Force (FONF, RG 24) file was routinely de-classified at the end of its fifty-year term. *The*

Department of National Defence subsequently released it to *Library and Archives Canada* who added it to their finding aids without fanfare.

One day, someone requested it.

THE END.

ABOUT THE AUTHOR

Photo by Rhonda Hayward/ *The Telegram*

PAUL W. COLLINS is a native Newfoundlander, with a doctoral degree in History from Memorial University of Newfoundland. He is a recognized consultant, speaker and author on Newfoundland during the Second World War and an expert on Newfyjohn's role in the Battle of the Atlantic.

Dr. Collins has contributed to such respected academic journals as *The Northern Mariner, Newfoundland and Labrador Studies* and *The*

Newfoundland Quarterly, as well as the *Heritage Newfoundland and Labrador* website.

In 2010, his essay "From Defended Harbour to Trans-Atlantic Base" on St. John's' development as a Second World War naval base appeared in the award-winning *Occupied St. John's: A Social History of a City at War 1939-1945* published by McGill-Queen's University Press. His own *The "Newfyjohn" Solution: St. John's, Newfoundland as a Case Study of Second World War Allied Naval Base Development During the Battle of the Atlantic* was released in 2014 and is the product of extensive research at the City of St. John's Archives; The Provincial Archives of Newfoundland and Labrador (PANL); Libraries and Archives Canada (LARC); and The National Archives (TNA/PRO), Kew, London, UK. Dangerous Waters is Dr. Collins' first novel.

www.drpaulwcollins.com